colin Bateman

reservoir Pups

D1392025

colin Bateman

reservoir Pups

Hodder
Children's
Books

a division of Hodder Headline Limited

For Matthew

A Catalogue record for this book is available
from the British Library

ISBN 0 340 87780 4

Typeset in Palatino by Avon DataSet Ltd,
Bidford-on-Avon, Warwickshire

Printed and bound in Great Britain by
Bookmarque Ltd., Croydon, Surrey

The paper and board used in this paperback by
Hodder Children's Books are natural recyclable products
made from wood grown in sustainable forests.
The manufacturing processes conform to the environmental
regulations of the country of origin.

Hodder Children's Books
a division of Hodder Headline Ltd
338 Euston Road
London NW1 3BH

One

Eddie's father was killed by dragons.

No, actually, that's a lie.

He was killed when his submarine exploded.

No, actually, that's a lie as well.

The absolute truth is that he was killed by aliens and his death was covered up by the government because it didn't want to frighten everyone.

Sorry – but that's not true either.

The absolute, absolute, hand on heart, swear to God truth is that he was murdered by terrorists.

Well, no, that's not it either.

The simple fact of the matter is that Eddie's dad wasn't dead at all. He wasn't dragon food, and he wasn't undergoing hideous experiments on one of Jupiter's moons. Eddie didn't even *wish* his dad was dead. It just sometimes felt like he was.

They had lived, quite happily, or so he had thought, in a small village on the coast of Ireland called Groomsport. It was a quaint little village, with just a couple of shops, a picturesque harbour and a creaky old church, and it was surrounded by lots of fields and woods, perfect for a boy to play in. His father worked as an engineer in the Belfast shipyard, and his mother as a nurse in the local health centre. Eddie went to the village school, he did reasonably well, he was happy.

HAPPY.

And then one day his mother came home from work and offered him a Jaffa cake.

Now, his mother never, ever, offered him a Jaffa cake, or indeed any sort of biscuit, because she was thinking of his teeth. She liked watching American television programmes where everyone had clean white teeth, and she wanted Eddie to have teeth like that when he grew up. She said it was too late for her own teeth, the damage was done, and so kept several packets of biscuits and numerous bars of chocolate hidden around the house for *her* to chew on after he had gone to bed, but there were none for him – there was still time to save Eddie's teeth, she maintained.

So Eddie *knew* something was up when she sat him down and offered him the Jaffa cake, and then when he had swallowed that first one, almost whole, in case she tried to take it back, she shook the packet at him and said, 'Have another.'

He took it, and blinked at her with his wide

brown eyes and said, 'What's wrong?' before taking a bite. Her face was pale and her eyes were red-rimmed, as if she'd been crying. He wouldn't normally have been concerned by this, because his mother always cried – at a dead cat on the road, at a baby bird falling out of its nest, at somebody getting terminally ill on *Coronation Street*, at somebody discovering a dusty old painting was worth thousands on the *Antiques Roadshow*, and sometimes when she ran out of cigarettes and the village shop was closed – but tears *and* Jaffa cakes together – well, it wasn't a good sign at all.

'I have good news and bad news, Eddie.'

Eddie took another bite of his Jaffa cake.

'Which do you want to hear first?'

Without thinking much about it, Eddie said, 'The good.'

Part of him was still hopeful that this would be something along the lines of she'd bought him a Walkman to listen to his CDs on, and the bad news was he'd have to spend his own pocket money to buy batteries. But most of him knew it wasn't going to be that straightforward.

'Okay – the good news is . . .' She took a deep breath. 'The good news is – I've got a new job, and we're moving to the city, and you'll have a wonderful new school and make lots of new friends.'

Eddie almost choked.

'*What?*' was the best he could manage.

'Yes,' she replied, blinking at him uncertainly. 'Isn't it wonderful? A new job, a whole new life, Eddie.'

'That's the good news?'

'Yes, dear.'

'THAT'S THE GOOD NEWS?'

'Now don't get upset, Eddie.'

'UPSET! You're making me leave my school, you're making me leave my friends, you're making me move to the city? And that's the *good* news! How could you? MUM, HOW COULD YOU?'

'Well,' his mum said rather weakly, 'that's just how it is.'

Eddie shook his head. 'And Dad agrees with this?'

His mother drummed her fingers nervously on the table. 'Well,' she said, '*that*'s the bad news.'

She reached across the table, took his hand and clasped it tightly. This was not a good idea, because it was the hand with the half-eaten Jaffa cake in it. The biscuit immediately began to melt, but Eddie didn't try to move his hand because he'd never seen his mother look so serious before.

'Eddie,' she said finally, 'I'm not going to beat about the bush here, I'm going to give it to you straight. I think you're old enough for me not to have to dress it all up in cotton wool like you're a little baby. You're a big boy now. Are you ready?'

Eddie nodded warily.

'First of all – your father has moved to Liverpool, and second of all, we're getting a divorce.'

'You're *what*?'

'We're getting a divorce.'

'You're *what*?'

'We're getting a divorce.'

'You're . . .'

'Eddie, there are only so many times I can say it. We're getting a divorce.'

'But, but, but, but, but . . .'

'I know it's a shock, and to tell you the truth it's a bit of a shock to me as well.' She sniffed, and sat a little more erect in her chair. 'While I was out at my night class, your father was having an affair with my good friend, my employer, the wonderful Dr Betty Armstrong.'

'You mean . . . Spaghetti Legs?'

'Yes, I mean Spaghetti Legs.'

'But . . . she's married.'

'Yes, Eddie, I know. But not for much longer.'

His mum was drumming her fingers on the table again. She had let go of his hand, and was unaware that her fingers were thick with melted chocolate.

Eddie stared at the cupboards. He stared at the sink. He stared at the floor and the ceiling and the window and the ceramic tiles and the wooden floor. He took a deep breath. He looked at his mother, who was also trying not to cry. This time he reached across and took *her* hand.

'So,' he said, clearing his throat, and trying to appear grown up about the whole situation, 'to paraphrase: Dad has run off with the doctor, because of that you've lost your job and have to move to the city to get a new one.'

Mum nodded.

'I have lost my father, my school, my friends, and my home, and I also have to move to the city, a city you have always said was dark and dangerous and never allowed me to go to.'

She nodded again. And then there were tears rolling down her cheeks. Eddie began to feel tears roll down his cheeks too.

Two

Eddie was bored. Bored, bored, bored, bored, bored.

Bored, bored, bored, bored, bored, bored.

Bored, bored, bored, bored, bored, bored. Bored.

'Well, why don't you go out and *do* something?' his mum said, pulling her coat on.

'Like what?' Eddie snapped. 'Play with the traffic?'

'Oh, I don't know. Something. And don't be so damn cheeky.'

She now worked as a nurse in the maternity wing of the Royal Victoria Hospital, which was as dark and dank as any building Eddie had ever been in. Hospitals were supposed to make you feel better, but this hospital made Eddie feel ill. But Mum seemed to like it. In fact, she seemed to like everything about her new life in the city, which worried Eddie, because he hated everything about it. He was completely and utterly bored, he hadn't spoken to anyone of his own age in three weeks, and he was spending most of his time staring out of the window of their apartment on the seventeenth floor of the nurses' quarters, which were right next to the hospital. This was handy for his mum, because she could stroll to work in a couple of minutes, but awful for Eddie because the hospital and the nurses' quarters were in a rough, tough part of the city, with a huge sprawling motorway on one side and a housing estate famous all over the world for being violent and dangerous on the other. It meant Eddie spent most of his time either watching TV – which was boring in itself because they couldn't afford cable and were stuck with just the normal rubbish channels – or hanging around the hospital, which was just as bad, because there were only so many sick people he could look at without starting to feel sick himself.

'I'll be back at lunch-time,' his mum said as she was going out the door, and then she paused for a moment, 'and I don't want you hanging around the hospital. It's not allowed. And I don't want you going down to the shops, because it's not safe. And try not to fall out the window, because it's seventeen floors down.'

'Well,' Eddie said, 'at least I'll be close to the hospital if I *do* fall out.'

His mum rolled her eyes. '*Please* try and cheer up, Eddie, things could be worse.'

After she was gone, Eddie tried to figure out exactly *how* things could be worse, him having no father, no friends, and nothing to do – but he very quickly got bored with that too. He stared at the traffic. He stared at the TV. He stared at the phone and wondered why his dad hadn't rung yet and then he thought that maybe his dad didn't have their new number, the same way that he didn't have his dad's new number. Eddie checked the telephone book and got the number for directory enquiries. He asked for the phone number of Edward Malone, his dad, in Liverpool and the lady on the phone said they had no number for an Eddie Malone in Liverpool and by the way do you have permission to use the phone because you sound like you're only about eight years old and Eddie snapped back that he was twelve, if it's any of your business, you old bag, and slammed the phone down. And then he thought he'd better go out in case she phoned back or decided to send round a squad of Telephone Engineers to beat him up.

They do say, when your life is a horrible mess,

that things can only get better, but it certainly didn't seem that way to Eddie. He had had a nice house, and a nice life, and he had a nice father, and they were a nice family, and suddenly he had none of the above. His mum told him the bad news on a Monday, and they moved the following Friday. He hardly even had time to say goodbye to his friends, and they didn't really know what to say to him, besides the usual things like 'keep in touch' and 'don't forget to give me that book back I lent you before you go'.

The Friday they moved was also the start of the summer holidays, and they were supposed to go to Spain for two weeks. When he raised the subject with his mum she got all tearful again, and he guessed that they weren't going, or that perhaps Dad and Spaghetti Legs were going instead.

Eddie took the elevator down to the ground floor, then wandered around the hospital grounds. He watched the ambulances arrive and disgorge their patients. He saw police escorting a man with a bandage round his head into the Casualty department screaming, 'I've been shot! I've been shot!' He saw three teenagers who'd been cut by glass when a bomb exploded. There had been violence of this kind going on in Belfast for as long as anyone could remember – it was called 'The Troubles'. Neighbour fought neighbour. Protestant fought Catholic. Gangsters fought gangsters. There was supposed to be some kind of peace agreement in place, but as far as Eddie could tell they were fighting over that as well. He saw a pregnant woman helped through the doors by her excited husband. He saw old people shuffling with the aid of walking sticks or rolling in on wheelchairs. He wandered through the car park looking at the cars, and felt nostalgic for Norman, which is what his dad, for no apparent reason, had called their car. Norman had taken them on all kinds of exciting trips. And now Norman was in Liverpool and if Eddie had to go anywhere he had to take the bus, although he never did have to go anywhere because his life was so boring.

Eddie was passing between the cars, kicking gravel, imagining what it would be like to be a patient in the hospital with some sort of interesting disease, like one that would make his head so enormous it would need scaffolding to support it, or one that would allow him to throw up whenever he felt like it, so he could fire it in any direction, the way Spiderman shot out his web, when he came across two boys of about his age scooping mud out of a puddle. As he watched, the boys turned with their handfuls of slime and threw them across the front of some nearby cars. They then lifted more mud from the puddle and began to move along the parking spaces, splattering as many vehicles as they could with the oozy, mucky mess.

One of the boys, with hair the colour of a ginger sponge cake and more freckles on his face than there are stars in the night sky, noticed that Eddie was watching and glared across at him. 'See enough?' he snapped.

Eddie nodded quickly and hurried on.

A woman, carrying several plastic bags, was now walking through the car park towards him. She nodded pleasantly and he smiled back. But she hadn't gone more than a few yards further along before she let out an angry shout. Eddie turned and saw that she'd dropped her bags and was staring at what was clearly her car, covered in mud. There was suddenly no sign of the two boys. Eddie, scared that he might get the blame, quickly ducked behind a parked Land-Rover. He only peered cautiously up when he heard voices, thinking perhaps that she had somehow caught the two boys responsible, but instead he saw that she was standing with a different boy, smaller, with close-cropped hair.

'Ah, missus,' the boy was saying, 'it's a dreadful state of affairs when you can't leave your car for ten minutes without this happening. And do you know, I think I saw the fella that done it.' The crop-haired boy pointed down the car park towards the Land-Rover. Eddie ducked down again, his face burning.

'Tell you what,' he heard the crop-haired boy say, 'I'll wash your car for you.'

'Well . . . I don't know,' the woman replied, 'I mean . . . how are you . . . ?'

'Missus, it's no problem.'

The crop-haired boy turned and let out a low whistle, and a moment later the ginger-haired boy and his accomplice came running up, one carrying a bucket of water, the other a sponge.

'My boys are the best in the business,' the crop-haired boy said as the other two came up beside him, grinning, 'and we just happen to be working in the neighbourhood. Wouldn't like to see a woman in distress now, would we? Come on, boys.'

And they immediately set to work washing her car.

'Why,' the woman said, 'that's very decent of you.'

'No problem at all now, missus,' the crop-haired boy said, standing back and supervising the work, 'and tell you what, we'll only charge you half our normal rate.'

'Oh . . . well, I thought . . . well, I suppose it needs doing, can't drive it in that condition, can I? My husband would have my guts for garters.'

The chancers. Eddie blew out his cheeks, then sneaked away along the row of cars, keeping his head down as low as he possibly could.

Three

Eddie was angrily plotting all kinds of revenge at being blamed for something he hadn't done. Why, he could be sent away to a home for doing something like that, or at the very least slapped in the chops by an angry woman. He'd sort them out, he'd phone the police, or tell the hospital security guards or . . . or . . . or . . .

. . . or he probably wouldn't do anything.

In fact, the further away from the boys he got, the more he realised it was quite a clever scam they were pulling. They weren't causing any real damage to the cars, so they weren't going to be arrested or anything, and most people were so vain about their cars they were prepared to pay a couple of pounds to get them cleaned up. Eddie sighed. He'd love to pull a scam like that, he just . . . well, he just didn't have the nerve for it.

As he approached the main doors of the hospital, with visitors arriving and leaving, nurses going home or starting their shifts, with patients-to-be limping in or former patients limping out, with taxis waiting and cars dropping off and picking up, Eddie became aware of a boy sitting in a wheelchair, rattling a small tin can with a slit in the top and repeating over and over: 'Help the disabled, help the disabled – thank you, love . . . help the disabled, help the disabled . . . thank you, missus . . .'

Eddie could see that the boy, who was sallow-faced and skinny as a rake, had a blanket across his legs and . . . well, he had a blanket across where his legs used to be. Clearly he no longer had legs. Slightly embarrassed, Eddie put his head down and began to hurry past.

'Hey, you!'

Eddie pretended he hadn't heard and marched on.

'HEY, YOU! Curly!'

Eddie stopped, suddenly affronted. He wasn't curly. He was the least curly person he knew. Not that he knew many people, not any more . . . Nevertheless. Curly, indeed.

'What do you mean, *Curly*?' he snapped back at the boy in the wheelchair. 'I'm not *curly*.'

The boy looked him over more carefully. 'Sorry. My mistake.' And his lips turned up into a sneer. 'What I meant was . . . *girly* . . .'

'You—' Eddie began, but he was quickly cut off.

'I saw you trying to sneak past, I saw you looking the other way, sneaking past like a little girly.'

'I wasn't—' Eddie began again.

'Yes, you were, you liar.' The boy held up his tin and rattled it violently. 'Help the disabled, help the disabled – come on, girly, help the disabled.'

Eddie wasn't quite sure what to do. He wasn't about to be goaded into handing over any money, but he also felt rather sorry for the lad, stuck in a wheelchair and all that. It couldn't be an easy life.

'Come on, girly.'

'I haven't any money.'

'Course you have.'

'I haven't. I really haven't.'

'Yes, you have. Everyone has money. Turn out your pockets.'

'No, I will not.'

'See.'

'I'm telling you, I haven't any—'

'Liar!'

This was really starting to annoy Eddie. He decided to just walk on and ignore him.

'Then give me your trainers.'

Eddie stopped again. '*What?*' he said.

'If you haven't any money, then give me your trainers.'

This was too much.

'What do you want trainers for,' Eddie snapped, 'if you haven't got any legs?'

As soon as he'd said it, Eddie knew it was the wrong thing to say.

The boy's mouth dropped open, and his eyes began to well up. 'I . . . I . . .' he began to say. 'I . . . I . . . could sell . . . them . . . donate . . . the money . . . to charity . . .'

And then he began to sob violently.

Eddie felt dreadful.

'You don't know what it's like,' the boy cried, 'sitting here all day in the cold and the rain . . . stuck in this wheelchair . . . I can't ride a bike, or climb a mountain . . . and then you come along and make fun of me . . .'

All around, people were stopping to find out what had made the disabled boy cry.

Eddie, his face burning, ventured forward. 'I'm s . . . sorry,' he stammered, 'I didn't mean to . . . Here . . . here . . .'

He knelt down and slipped his trainers off without untying them. They were quite new. In fact they were one of the last things his father had bought him before he'd run off with Spaghetti Legs. But, instinctively, Eddie knew that this was the right thing to do. He lifted the trainers and held them out to the boy.

'I'm sorry,' he said, 'please take them.'

The boy dragged the sleeve of his jacket across his face, then nodded and took the trainers out of Eddie's hands.

Just at that moment there came an angry shout from within the hospital building. The disabled boy looked startled for a moment, then glanced back through the doors and along the main corridor.

'Scuttles!' the disabled boy hissed, then threw off his blanket and leapt out of his wheelchair. He stood for several moments on two perfectly good and functioning legs, then took off at speed away from the hospital and through the car park. As he ran, he was joined by the crop-haired boy, the ginger sponge boy and the other car-washer and together they raced out of the hospital grounds, laughing hysterically.

Between them they were carrying a bucket, a sponge, a tin full of change, quite a lot of money for washing dirty cars – and Eddie's trainers.

Eddie didn't know whether to laugh or cry.

And he didn't have time to decide because, before he knew what was happening, he was lifted off his feet and slammed hard against the hospital wall by a large man wearing a black uniform and a very angry expression.

Four

'I'm sick to death of little rats like you!' Scuttles roared. 'If it was up to me, I'd exterminate the lot of you!'

Eddie stared at the ground. Scuttles or, as it said on his name badge, Bernard J. Scuttles, Head of Security, stomped back and forth in front of Eddie, ranting and raging. If it was ever possible for steam to literally come out of a human's ears, Eddie was quite certain it would choose to come out of Mr Scuttles'. He was furious.

They were in Scuttles' office on the fourth floor of the hospital. It was part of an office suite which also included two rooms packed with a bewildering variety of surveillance equipment with which Scuttles and his team of sixteen security guards kept a constant watch on the comings and goings inside the hospital buildings and outside in the hospital grounds and car parks.

He was a large man – not fat, but well-built and muscular – with thick lips and penetrating eyes which made Eddie shiver every time he looked into them. Eddie kept his eyes on the ground and wished this would end.

'Don't you think I've got better things to do than watch little rats like you vandalise my hospital?'

'I wasn't—'

'Be quiet!'

Eddie was quiet. He'd tried explaining about the disabled boy and the trainers, and for good measure started to tell him about the boys pulling the scam in the car park, but Scuttles didn't want to know.

'We are working ourselves into the ground for Miss Beech's visit, our security has to be as tight as a drum, next Friday will be the most important day in the history of this hospital, and we don't need little rats like you sneaking about stealing things . . .'

'I wasn't—'

'Be quiet! Or I swear to God I'll have you locked up and I'll throw away the key!'

Eddie had no idea who Miss Beech was or why she was so important, and frankly, he didn't much care. All he wanted was to be out of there. He would quite happily never darken the grounds of the hospital again.

There was a knock on the door, and another

security guard stepped in. He was taller than Scuttles, thinner. Eddie couldn't help but notice a very distinctive pair of snakeskin cowboy boots poking out from the bottom of his uniform trousers. It made him look kind of rugged, like he'd just stepped off the set of a Western movie. 'Mr Scuttles,' he said in a surprisingly soft voice, 'the boy's mother is here.'

Scuttles himself glanced down at the cowboy boots and rolled his eyes. 'I've told you about those,' he snapped. The Cowboy shrugged. 'Okay,' Scuttles said, 'wheel her in.'

Oh, great, Eddie thought.

She didn't stop talking about it for hours. 'I have a new job, I'm trying to make a good impression, I'm trying to better myself, and you – and all you can do is get yourself into trouble, and then they call me out of a most important training meeting, oh, the embarrassment of it, the shame . . .'

'I didn't do—'

'Be quiet!'

Eddie was sent to his room. He was forbidden to leave the apartment for the next three days, he was forbidden to watch TV, and he was most certainly forbidden to go near the hospital.

On the second day of his punishment, his mum came home at lunch-time and gave him a Power Rangers action figure.

'I'm sorry, love,' she said.

Eddie, not sure what was up with her, why she was suddenly being friendly again, held the figure at arm's length, slightly embarrassed. He was a bit old for Power Rangers action figures.

Mum made herself a cup of tea and sat down at the table. She shook a packet of Jaffa cakes at him. Eddie took one warily and sat down opposite her.

'What's wrong, Mum?'

Maybe *she* was leaving too. Maybe he would be put in an orphanage.

'Nothing's wrong, sweetpea,' she said, reaching across to take his hand, although this time he was alert enough to switch the Jaffa cake so she wouldn't squish it. 'It's just . . . well, I've been very hard on you. I know it's not easy, being in a new city, trying to meet new friends. It's very easy to fall in with the wrong type of boy. You just need to be more careful.'

'Mum – they weren't my friends. I didn't even know them. I was just in the wrong place at the wrong time.'

'Well. What's done is done, and you'll know better next time.'

Eddie sighed. He wasn't really getting through to her. But at least she was in better form now. Things could get back to normal. Boring, boring normal. Eddie sighed again. His mum squeezed his hand. 'Mr Scuttles was telling me all about the terrible trouble he has with gangs of boys around the hospital, he says it's like the Wild West.'

'Yes, Mum.'

'I don't want you hanging around with them. You're a good boy, you don't want to go getting yourself into trouble again.'

'No, Mum.'

'It reflects badly on me.'

'Yes, Mum.'

She sat back then, letting go of his hand. She smiled to herself and said, 'I'm quite excited, actually.'

'Excited about what?'

'The lottery.'

'You mean the lottery on TV?'

'No, silly, the lottery at work.'

'What lottery at work?'

'Oh, Eddie, don't you ever listen? I told you all about it. They're going to draw out six names, six nurses who'll get to meet her. Fingers crossed, eh?'

'Meet who, Mum?'

She laughed. 'Who? Alison Beech *who*. Honestly, Eddie, sometimes I think you live on another planet.'

Eddie rubbed at his brow. 'Mum. I do live on another planet. Earth, it's called. You must call in next time you visit. Now, who is Alison Beech?'

His mum looked at him incredulously. 'Who is Alison Beech? *Who* is Alison Beech? Honest to God, Eddie . . .' Suddenly she jumped up out of her chair and grabbed Eddie's hand. 'Come on, son, I'll introduce you.'

She began to lead him across the kitchen.

'Mum, what are you—'

'Come on . . . let's meet Alison Beech.'

He tried to resist, but she kept pulling him, along the hall, towards the bathroom.

'Mum, have you gone off your rocker?'

'Don't be shy, Eddie, let's meet . . .' – and she flung open the bathroom door with a flourish – 'Ladies and gentlemen,' she exclaimed, 'may I present . . . Miss Alison Beech!'

Eddie saw the bath with the hairs in the bottom nobody had washed out, the sink with the toothpaste cap lodged in the plughole, the open door of the bathroom cabinet with the jumble of his mum's half-finished lotions and potions, the toilet which someone – well, Eddie – had forgotten to flush. But no one or no thing that could possible be described as Alison Beech.

'Mum,' Eddie said, 'you're barking.'

But she wasn't to be put off. She waved across the room. 'Alison Beech,' she said.

'Mum,' Eddie said calmly, 'there's nobody there.'

'Oh, *Eddie*,' Mum said, 'open your eyes.'

She crossed to the bathroom cabinet and began lifting down her bottles and tubes of creams and make-up. 'Look, Eddie,' she said, holding them out to him one after the other, 'Alison Beech Moisturiser For Normal Skin, Alison Beech No.3 Eyeliner, Alison Beech Shampoo for Greasy Hair, Alison Beech . . .'

She could quite happily have reeled off the many and varied Alison Beech products she possessed for the next five minutes.

'All right, all right!' said Eddie. 'I get the picture. She does make-up, what's the big deal?'

Mum looked exasperated. 'She doesn't *do make-up*, Eddie, she changes our lives, she makes us feel as young and beautiful as she is, she's the most gorgeous, powerful, charismatic . . . oh, she's just

27

so wonderful . . . and she's coming to our little hospital!'

'Why, is she sick?'

'No, she's not sick!' Mum half-exploded. 'Honestly, Eddie, you've got to get out more. Alison Beech is the richest woman in Ireland, possibly the world, and she's coming to *our* hospital to give us ten million pounds to open a new wing. Oh, she's just lovely, and if my name comes out of the hat, *I'll* get to meet her, *I'll* get to show her round the hospital. Isn't that *fantastic*?'

'Yes, Mum,' said Eddie.

Five

Eddie's mum banned him from setting foot in the hospital grounds.

Naturally, the first thing he did when he was allowed out of the apartment was to go straight back there. Actually, it was the second thing he did. The first thing he did was to find out if the Power Rangers action figure could fly. He did this by dropping it out of the window. It fell seventeen floors and smashed to smithereens on the ground below, thus proving that despite its great fighting ability, it could not, in fact, fly.

Over the next few days Eddie explored the hospital from top to bottom. It was kind of exciting, doing something he was expressly forbidden to do. There were eighteen different floors, each one served by half a dozen elevators and two different sets of stairs. There were floors for old people, for very, very, very, very, very sick people, there was a children's floor, there was a floor for people with diseases that were so infectious that you had to wear special clothes to enter it, there was a floor

29

for women to go and have their babies, there was a floor where all the mad people were kept with a big locked door and a security guard in front of it to stop any of them escaping and boiling cats or eating soil, and there was even a basement where they kept the dead bodies before they were taken away for burial. There were two restaurants – one for patients and visitors, one for the nurses and doctors – there were kitchens where vast vats of soup and custard simmered day and night, there were laundries where sheets thick with fleas and scabs and excrement were cleaned or burned in great furnaces which also fed a huge bubbling, churning boiler which heated the entire hospital. And there was, of course, the security centre, where Scuttles kept an eye on everything. Eddie learned where the cameras were in each corridor, which areas they covered, and which areas they missed; there were so many cameras, one in every corridor, one in every ward, that they couldn't all be watched all the time, and he soon learned that when a red light was flashing on one of the cameras, mounted high on the walls, that meant that that camera was 'hot' and was being watched in the security centre. When the light wasn't flashing, he was free to patrol that area.

Two or three times he nearly ran into Scuttles as he did his rounds, and once Scuttles walked right past him without noticing. Eddie breathed a sigh of relief. Scuttles' mind was elsewhere – in fact, *everyone* who worked at the hospital seemed to have their minds elsewhere, because Alison Beech was coming.

Everyone was so excited.

Everything was being brushed and freshly painted: the walls, the ceilings, the doors, even some of the patients.

Pictures of Alison Beech were put up, banners were hung, bunting was strung across the corridors. It almost felt like Christmas in the summer.

Alison Beech was coming!

Eddie, of course, was thoroughly bored by Alison Beech, and not impressed at all. So she did make-up. And everyone spent a fortune on it. Eddie had seen the price stickers on his mum's tubes and ointments, and they weren't cheap. Eddie could think of a hundred better things his mum could be spending her money on: cable TV for a start, and new trainers wouldn't go amiss. He'd been wearing his old manky pair for over a week now, and he could almost feel his toes pointing through the end of them, they were so worn out.

But no, she'd rather slap some Alison Beech on her face.

Eddie was just leaving the hospital after another fruitful day of exploring – he'd discovered the freezers where the food was kept and a small room full of jars where little body parts were preserved, like eyes and toes and ears – when he heard . . . well, not a familiar voice exactly, but a familiar cry.

'Help the disabled! Help the disabled! Thank you very much, missus!'

The entrance to the hospital was as busy as ever and it took Eddie a moment or two to locate the source of the cry. But then two elderly women turned away, having deposited some coins in the outstretched tin, and Eddie saw a different boy sitting in a different wheelchair, but shaking the same kind of tin.

'Help the disabled! Help the disabled!' he cried.

He had the same kind of sallow look on his face, and he had a tartan rug across his legs – not that he *had* any legs, of course.

Hah!

Eddie, who was becoming increasingly bold

as his confidence in his new surroundings grew, marched right up to him.

'You've got a right nerve!' he said.

'Excuse me?' the boy replied.

'I said, you've got a right nerve. Who do you think you are, sitting there, shaking your little tin, ripping people off like that?'

'What are you talking about?'

'You know fine well, you bloody chancer. You and your gang – you got me locked up in my room for three days, do you know that?'

'I've never seen you before in my life. Now go away and let me get on with my work.'

'Your work! You're a con man, and I'll have security on you.'

'Ah bog off, wee lad!'

And that really got Eddie. He'd show him. He'd show him okay.

Eddie suddenly slapped the tin of money out of the boy's hands. It hit the ground half a dozen yards away. The top sprang off it and maybe a hundred coins spilled across the rough cement.

'You—!' the boy began, but Eddie, a wild temper on him now, wasn't finished.

He reached behind the boy, grabbed hold of the wheelchair, spun it round, then using all

33

his strength, tipped it up and spilled the boy out of it.

The boy tumbled forward on to the ground with a shout which was a mixture of surprise, anger and pain.

He rolled over twice. The tartan blanket fell away from him. All around people were stopping, shocked at the vision of this poor disabled lad being thrown out of his wheelchair by an obviously deranged street urchin.

'Oh!' an old woman exclaimed. 'You bad little bugger!'

Eddie half laughed, raising his hands to calm her down. 'No, you don't understand,' he began.

But the woman backed away, frightened. 'Keep away from me!' she said, clearly terrified.

'No, listen . . . listen,' Eddie said, aware that more and more people were stopping to watch. 'There's nothing wrong with him, he's not disabled, he's only pretend—'

And, as Eddie pointed down at the boy lying on the ground, crying now, he realised that, actually, he *didn't* have any legs. He really *was* . . .

Eddie, his heart thumping, his stomach dropping into his feet, started to back away. 'I . . . I . . . I . . .

I . . . I . . .' He was trying to say something, trying to apologise, to take it back and make things better, but he knew he couldn't, it was too late, he had to get out of there, he had to run away and hide. He turned . . .

But his way was blocked. By a black, heaving, towering presence.

Two huge hands reached down, grabbed his jumper and lifted him off the ground.

'You little *rat*,' it hissed at him.

Scuttles.

Six

'This time I have you, I really have you!'

Scuttles was stomping up and down in front of Eddie, his eyes ablaze, his voice harsh and rasping, his mouth flecked with spit. They were in a small, bare room off the security centre – there was a desk, a chair, an ashtray and a single light bulb. The room smelled of cigarettes and sweat.

'The police are on their way. They're going to arrest you. They're going to charge you with assaulting that poor lad, they're going to charge you with attempting to steal his money, they're going to put you away, and it's no more than you deserve, you little gutter rat. You're the worst yet, attacking that poor little ... oh!' Scuttles threw up his hands in anger. Then he stomped towards the door. 'I don't even want to be in the same room with you!' He pulled the door open, then jabbed an ugly, fat finger back at Eddie. 'You and your gang, your days are numbered! Now sit there and shut up, I'll be back with the police.'

Scuttles left the room, slamming then locking the door behind him.

Eddie lowered his head on to the table.

This time he had done it, he had really done it.

And there were no excuses.

He was guilty.

He had attacked a disabled boy. He had hurled him out of his wheelchair. Thrown him on to the ground with such force that he would probably have broken his legs, if he'd had any. A boy wearing a big sticker which said he had official permission to collect money for charity in the grounds of the hospital. A big yellow sticker Eddie had missed completely.

How could he have been so stupid? Why had he lost his temper like that? What would the police do to him? How many different ways was his mother going to kill him? He would need to get a lawyer. There would be a big trial. He would be in all the newspapers. He would be known all over the country as the boy who attacked disabled children and stole their money. He would be expelled from his new school before he even had a chance to attend. All his friends would despise him – although he didn't have any friends. Complete strangers would hurl abuse, and stones at him. He was despicable.

What was he to do?

Even now the police were probably parking outside, coming up the elevator, getting the handcuffs ready.

Would he cry and plead with them not to take him away? 'It was a mistake, an honest to goodness mistake, I wouldn't do something like that, I couldn't do . . .'

And then Scuttles would come in with a videotape taken from one of the security cameras which would show Eddie throwing the poor disabled lad out of his wheelchair. The police would drag him out by his feet or his ears or his hair, with the whole hospital looking at him, and his mother crying hysterically.

Eddie buried his face in his hands and groaned.

Then he heard the key in the door.

This was it, then.

Off to prison.

The door opened. Eddie shut his eyes tight, desperately trying to convince himself that it was all a dream while knowing all the time that it was worse than that. It was a nightmare.

But the voice, when it came, was totally unexpected.

'Hey, Curly, let's move.'

Eddie turned to the door. The disabled boy who wasn't disabled. The boy who'd stolen his trainers. He was standing in the doorway grinning nervously.

'C'mon!' the boy said. 'We haven't got all day.'

'But—' Eddie began.

'Do you want out, or do you want to wait for the cops?'

'But—'

The boy gave Eddie an exasperated look. Then there was movement beside him and the boy with the ginger hair peered in. 'What's the hold-up?'

'Laughing boy here can't make his mind up. Will you come *on*?'

And then there was a crackle of static and the ginger boy lifted what looked to Eddie like a walkie-talkie to his ear, exactly the sort of communication device he'd noticed pinned to Scuttles' chest. A voice said: 'They're in the lift.'

Ginger nodded, then looked across at Eddie: 'This is your last chance,' he said.

Eddie's heart was pounding in his chest. Who were these boys? What were they playing at, why were they helping him, why was—

'Will you make your bloody mind up!'

Eddie suddenly jumped to his feet and dashed across the room towards them. What did he have to lose? A life on the run was better than life in prison. He squeezed past the boys into the corridor.

The boy who had been disabled closed the door behind them and locked it, using one of a dozen keys on a key-ring which he then slipped back into a small bag he carried over his shoulder.

Eddie started to move down the corridor to the left.

'No!' Ginger snapped. 'This way.'

All three of them turned to the right and started running. Just as they reached the end of the corridor, the elevator doors opened at the opposite end. Eddie couldn't help but glance back to see Scuttles, the security guard with the grey cowboy boots, and several police officers, emerging from it before Ginger bundled him on around the corner.

They paused for a moment, Ginger sneaking a look back at Scuttles and the police as they entered the Security Centre. Moments later there came an angry roar. Ginger turned back to them, smiling. 'Come on!' he said.

Eddie ran with them, pushed through swing doors on to the stairs, taking them three at a time.

Then the boy who had been disabled stopped

them suddenly as they turned the corner on to the next flight of stairs.

'Security camera!' he hissed.

Eddie knew all about the security cameras. Breathing hard, he said, 'If the red light is—'

'We know about the red lights, Curly,' the boy snapped back, before inching around the corner. 'It's off,' he said, and then led the way again as they raced down the stairs.

Five minutes later, the three of them were standing, almost bent double, trying to catch their breath, outside the hospital grounds, just on the edge of the vast, gloomy housing estate Eddie had eyed warily from his lofty apartment. He wasn't sure if he particularly liked these boys, but they'd certainly got him out of a jam.

As he caught his breath, Eddie did his best to smile at them. 'I . . . well, thanks for doing that. I mean, how . . . why would you . . . where did you get the keys . . . and . . .'

Ginger took another deep breath, then straightened. 'We have the keys for every room in that place.'

'But how – and why?'

'Because it's our territory.'

'What do you mean, *territory*?'

'It belongs to the Pups,' the ex-disabled boy said.

'The pups? What do you mean, the pups?'

Ginger looked at him, disbelief etched on his face. 'You've never heard of the Pups?'

Eddie shook his head.

'You've never heard of the Reservoir Pups?'

'Uh . . . no. Sorry.'

'The Reservoir Pups are the most feared gang in this whole city, and that hospital is right in the middle of our patch. Now do you understand?'

'Right. Right. Uh, no, not really. I'm kind of . . . new in town.'

Ginger shook his head. 'Okay. Put simply, we own this part of the city, nothing moves, nothing happens, nobody does nothing unless we know about it, and we say it's okay. Okay?'

'Okay,' Eddie said.

'This hospital, it's one of our main sources of income. And anyone tries to interfere with that, well, they're in big trouble. Scuttles, he's our enemy number one. Anything we can do to annoy him, well, that's what we'll do. That's why we got you out. He'll be bloody furious.'

The two Reservoir Pups laughed and punched each other hard on the arm. Eddie laughed too, but decided not to risk punching either of them. 'Well,' he said, eventually, 'thanks anyway.' He glanced down at his watch. 'I, uh . . . well, I suppose I should get home. Cheers again. And I'll, uh, see you around.'

Eddie nodded at them, then turned to go.

But Ginger was suddenly blocking his way. He placed the palm of his hand firmly on Eddie's chest. 'You've to come with us,' he said bluntly. 'Captain Black wants to see you.'

'Captain . . . ?' Eddie began. 'I don't . . . I mean, look, some other time maybe, I really *do* have to get home.'

Eddie took a step back, but his way was blocked again, this time by the ex-disabled boy, who took a firm hold of the back of his shirt.

'I don't think you understand, Curly,' the boy hissed, 'you're ours. You're a prisoner of the Reservoir Pups.'

Seven

They pushed and prodded him, all the time leading him deeper and deeper into the Rivers, the darkest, dankest housing estate in Belfast. The roads were covered in broken glass, the walls in graffiti, discarded tyres were burning, houses were boarded up – it looked like a war zone Eddie had seen on TV. In fact, it *was* a war zone Eddie had seen on TV and now he was being led into the very heart of it.

He didn't go without a struggle, he tried to escape. He bent to tie his lace, and from his kneeling position suddenly took off, but they caught him within twenty metres. Then he tried to be all chummy, hoping they'd feel sympathetic towards him, and let him go, but while they nodded and smiled like they cared, they just kept nudging him forwards towards . . . well, he had no idea, and he didn't like it one little bit.

The ex-disabled boy called his friend Bap. And Bap called his friend Bacon. As they walked, they encountered other kids standing in small groups on street corners. Bap would give a hand signal and a similar signal would be returned, then they'd keep walking on into the Rivers. Eddie felt like he was being led into a very large, very busy and very dangerous ant hill and that very soon he would meet the King of the Ants himself, and be eaten.

Eventually they came to a dark narrow street almost entirely made up of boarded-up houses. There was a burned-out car at one end and an empty shop at the other. In between the two there were perhaps a dozen terraced houses on each side. Eddie had the feeling that he could scream and scream here, and nobody would hear him. Bap and Bacon marched him halfway up, then stopped at a front door which was protected by a metal grille; they glanced both ways, then rapped three times on the grille, paused for a moment, then repeated the knocking another three times. After perhaps thirty seconds the door opened a fraction, and a voice said: 'Flash.'

'Thunder,' Bap replied and the door was opened fully by a tall boy wearing a red zip jacket and a baseball cap.

'You got him.'

Bacon nodded and pushed Eddie through the door.

The house may have looked abandoned from the outside, but inside it was a hive of activity. Instead of furniture there was computer equipment, instead of paintings on the wall there were maps, instead of stairs there were ramps. As he was led through the house he saw rooms packed with cardboard boxes, most were sealed, but others were half open: he saw CDs, DVDs, toasters, lamps, all being checked by a boy with a clip board; he saw a room where money was being counted, a larger room where boys were being led through a series of exercises. In fact, as he continued to walk, Eddie realised that he was no longer in the same house – that part of the dividing wall with the next house, and then the next and the next had been removed, giving the Reservoir Pups a headquarters which covered four terraced houses. It was both very impressive and very scary.

Eventually he was stopped before a closed door towards the back of the headquarters; Bap pressed a buzzer, then stepped back and looked up at the ceiling. Eddie followed his gaze and saw a small security camera. After a slight delay the buzzer sounded again and the door swung automatically open. Bap took hold of Eddie's arm, making him stay where he was while Bacon entered, marching directly up to a boy sitting with his back to the door, facing a computer screen.

'Captain Black,' Bacon said, 'we have the prisoner.'

The boy nodded slowly, without taking his eyes off the screen. 'Any problems?' he asked, with a kind of vague indifference. Yet there was something familiar about his voice.

'No, sir, everything went according to plan.'

Then Eddie realised that the boy was sitting in a wheelchair. And he suddenly felt very uneasy indeed.

The wheelchair began to turn, and Bacon stepped out of its path, allowing Eddie and the Captain their first view of each other.

Well, their first view since earlier that afternoon.

The boy with no legs. The boy he had thrown out of his wheelchair.

Bap thrust Eddie forwards into the room. He came to a halt and stood staring at this Captain Black, sweat dripping down his back, his legs weak at the knees.

Then the leader of the Reservoir Pups looked Eddie up and down, his eyes narrowed and he hissed: 'Attacked any disabled kids lately?'

Eddie swallowed hard.

Eight

Eddie began to stammer out a reply, but Captain Black held up a hand and said, 'Relax.' Then he nodded at Bacon and Bap and they both left the room, closing the door behind them. Eddie was utterly confused. He couldn't believe he was alone with this disabled boy, whom he'd left crying and moaning on the ground outside the hospital not more than a couple of hours ago, and who was now here, lording it over a gang that seemed to control huge swathes of the city.

'I . . . don't . . . understand,' Eddie said weakly.

'What don't you understand?' Captain Black asked.

Eddie shrugged helplessly. 'Everything,' he said. Then he added quickly, 'But I'm really sorry about . . . earlier . . . You know, I didn't mean to . . . to hurt you.'

Captain Black glared at Eddie for several long moments, but then his face softened into a smile. 'You didn't,' he said, then nodded at a plastic chair on his left. 'Have a seat, Eddie. I know this must all seem very strange for you.'

Eddie sat. He nodded. Then ventured: 'Why have you brought me here?'

'Well,' said Captain Black, 'I wanted to meet the man who dared to throw the leader of the Reservoir Pups out of his wheelchair.'

'I told you, I didn't mean—'

'*Shhhh.*'

Eddie *shhhhhd*.

'I understand you're new to this area.' Eddie nodded. Black turned and hit a key on his computer. Immediately a photograph of Eddie appeared on screen. 'You live at apartment 1709 in the nurses' block, you're enrolled at Grosvenor Secondary School, your dad has left home.'

'How—'

Black smiled round at him. 'I know everything, Eddie. It's my job. Information, Eddie, if you have access to the right sort, can help you achieve anything. For example, I was able to hack into the hospital's mainframe computer and lift out information about your mother and where she lives, I was able to feed your name into the Education Department's master files and find out what school you're going to. And the photograph was lifted from Scuttles' security cameras, which we have a direct feed from.' Black hit another button and immediately Eddie was looking at the inside of Scuttles' security office. In fact he could see Scuttles sitting at his desk, eating a doughnut.

Eddie couldn't help but edge forward in his seat. 'That's *fantastic*,' he said.

'Yeah,' said Captain Black, 'it is pretty cool.'

Black hit another key, and Scuttles disappeared from the screen. Eddie sat back in his chair. 'But . . .'

'Why?'

Eddie nodded.

'Because with the right information, you stay ahead of the field, and that's what we have to do to survive.'

'Survive?' Eddie said.

Black looked at him for several uncomfortable moments, then shook his head sadly. 'I forgot,' he said, 'you're not from the city. You don't really know what it's like, do you?'

'Well, I . . .' Eddie began bravely, then shook his head. 'Not really, no.'

Captain Black clasped his hands in front of his face for several moments, nodding to himself, then looked back up at Eddie. 'Eddie,' he said, 'Belfast is a tough place to live. People have been fighting with each other here for as long as we've been alive, for as long as our parents have been alive.'

Eddie nodded. He knew that, though kind of vaguely. He didn't really pay much attention to the news on TV.

'And here in the Rivers, there's been more fighting than almost anywhere else. Most of the kids round here, their parents are either dead or they're in prison. Most of those who're still alive, or not inside, they have no jobs, because nobody wants to employ someone from the Rivers, or they're too sick to work, or some of them are just too lazy. So if you're a kid you can either sit back and accept that, or you can do something about it. We decided to do something about it.'

'The Reservoir Pups,' said Eddie.

'Exactly. You ever heard of Robin Hood, Eddie?'

Eddie nodded.

'You remember what they said about him? What his catchphrase was?'

'He steals from the rich, and gives to the poor.'

'Yeah, that's it. Well, we're a bit like that. We steal from the rich – and we keep it.'

'I see.'

'We're not criminal, Eddie, we're just trying to survive.'

Eddie nodded, then added: 'You . . . uh, seem to be surviving very well.'

Captain Black laughed suddenly. 'Yes, we are.' He nodded to himself for a moment, then let the smile slip from his face. 'The important thing is, Eddie, we all work for each other, we are all sworn to protect the gang. We have a lot of enemies out there – Scuttles for one, in fact most every adult you care to come across, and then there are the other gangs. You know about the other gangs?'

Eddie shook his head.

Captain Black turned back to the computer, and hit another key. Immediately a colour map of the city appeared on the screen, with areas shaded in red, green and blue.

'The green areas,' Captain Black said, moving his finger across the screen, 'are areas controlled by gangs loyal to the Alliance, which is an agreement between a number of gangs not to enter each other's territory without permission, to respect each other's gang members, i.e. no fighting or stealing from each other, and it's also an agreement through which we co-operate on certain military operations. Here for example,' he said, tapping one part of the city, 'we have the Ramsey Street Wheelers, here there are the Donegal

Road Retrievers, over here we have the Church Hill Regulars – there're about a dozen gangs in all. The red areas, now they're controlled by gangs who aren't loyal to the Alliance, they don't help anyone but themselves and don't think anything of stealing from another gang, or crossing into their territory, or attacking them. They're as hard as nails, and if you know what's good for you, you'll keep out of their way.' He touched the screen again. 'Here, for instance, down by the docks, there's the Strand Road Agitators. Here, there's the Andytown Albinos. You don't want to mess with them.'

Eddie nodded at the screen. 'And the blue area? What gangs are there?'

Captain Black shook his head sadly. 'Eddie, that's the river. There are no gangs there. They'd drown.'

Eddie laughed, embarrassed.

Captain Black turned then and clasped his hands in his lap. 'So, Eddie,' he said, 'that's what we're up to. Now, what about you?'

Eddie, who'd been starting to relax, suddenly felt a little shaky again. 'What do you mean?' he asked warily.

'Well,' said Captain Black, 'you're either with us, or against us. It's not safe for you out there all by yourself. If you join us, you'll have the support of the organisation, you'll have friends for life, you'll earn good money, and you'll have our protection. So, are you going to join us, Eddie?'

Eddie looked at Captain Black. He looked at the computer screen with its glowing map of Belfast, he thought of the network of houses the gang was based in, he thought of its computer screens and monitors and its members training together, he thought of the pang of envy he'd experienced watching the boys pull off their scam in the car park, and the excitement of breaking out of Scuttles' grasp and making their bid for freedom. And he thought of the utter boredom of sitting in his apartment, without a friend in the world.

Eddie took a deep breath. 'I'd love to join,' he said.

Captain Black reached out and shook his hand. 'And we'll be pleased to have you. All you have to do now is pop outside and Bacon will explain your mission.'

'My mission?' Eddie said, surprised.

'Yes, Eddie, your mission. You don't think we just let *anyone* join the Reservoir Pups, do you? You have to prove yourself, you know.'

Nine

Eddie was escorted to the edge of the Rivers estate by two boys he didn't know and who barely spoke to him, then tramped on by himself the rest of the way to the nurses' block just inside the hospital grounds. He took the lift to the seventeenth floor then let himself into the apartment. He wasn't sure exactly how he felt. Part of him was really excited at the prospect of joining the Reservoir Pups. But most of him was absolutely terrified. What had he been thinking of, saying he would join up? They were a gang of street kids, tough kids who ran wild across the city, stealing and pulling scams, kids his mum would kill him for hanging around with, kids who were going to end up in prison or dead or both, just like their parents.

Eddie made himself a sandwich, then sat with it by the window, staring out over the city. It was getting dark and his mum wasn't home yet. The sandwich tasted like cardboard. He hated Belfast. He wanted to go home to Groomsport. He wanted to play with his friends in the fields. He wanted to climb in the trees. He wanted his dad. He wanted to tell his dad about the gang. He wanted to ask him what he should do: whether he should join the Reservoir Pups, whether he should go on his mission.

The mission was what worried him most of all. It was so dangerous and stupid. Who would be thick enough to break into the hospital security centre, and steal all the security codes? What complete fool would attempt that? Throwing mud on cars was one thing. Pretending to be disabled was another. But burglary. Theft.

Yet he had agreed to do it.

In front of all the Reservoir Pups he had held up his hand and promised to do it. Like a fool.

He had felt it was wrong even then, had been scared in their presence – ranks and ranks of them staring at him, threatening him – but he had also felt excited: excited to be part of such an organisation, a member of such a gang. He had got caught up in the adventure of being sent on a dangerous mission without even thinking about the practicalities, the reality of having to break into Scuttles' private computer.

Part of him feared that they didn't really want or need him as a Reservoir Pup, that they were merely using him, that even if he succumbed to this madness, they might just take the codes off him and throw him back out on the street again.

Eddie sighed.

What choice did he really have? They had given him a small black button which they had stuck on to his jacket and told him was a tracking device. He was to carry it with him at all times so that they would always know where he was. It would also identify him to gang members and to other gangs from the Alliance – but without it, he would surely get a hammering. If he ever went out again, that was. What a choice! He tried to remember the names of some of the other gangs in the Alliance: the Donegal Road Retrievers, that was one – and the Church Hill Regulators, that was another. But there were dozens of them he couldn't remember or didn't know. And what if he unwittingly stumbled into an area controlled by a gang that *wasn't* part of the Alliance – like the Andytown Albinos? Eddie shivered. The city had seemed dark and dangerous before he had even ventured out into it, but now the reality of it was ten times worse than he'd imagined.

Maybe it wasn't too late. He could go and see

Captain Black and tell him he'd had second thoughts, that after due consideration he'd decided that the Reservoir Pups weren't for him. He would join the Scouts instead. Captain Black was sure to understand.

No, Eddie thought, he was sure *not* to understand. Captain Black had said that joining the Pups was all about loyalty and friendship, and Eddie had held up his hand and promised to undertake the mission. If he backed out now, he would not only be breaking his promise, he would also be making enemies of the Reservoir Pups, the gang that ruled the very streets where he lived.

Eddie rubbed his brow. He had the beginnings of a headache. Who was Captain Black, anyhow? Eddie had been so concerned with his own predicament, he hadn't stopped to ask how a boy with no legs could come to be the leader of such a large and dangerous gang.

Eddie turned at the sound of the front door opening. Mum. Giggling to herself about something, blissfully unaware of Eddie's predicament. He hoped she didn't ask him what sort of a day he'd had. 'Oh, the usual,' Eddie would say. 'I attacked a disabled boy, threw him out of his wheelchair, then nearly got arrested by the police, but managed to break out of the security centre and escape. Then I swore to undertake a dangerous and illegal mission on behalf of a band of outlaws. How was your day?'

Except that now he realised that Mum wasn't giggling to herself, she was standing half in, half out of the front door, laughing and chatting with somebody else. 'Come on in, don't be silly,' she was saying, and then she giggled again. She stepped back out into the hall and beckoned whoever it was in, then caught a glance of Eddie. 'Oh, Eddie,' she said, 'I wasn't sure if you'd be home. We have a visitor.' She smiled towards the door again, then back at Eddie as her guest entered the apartment. 'Eddie, I think you've already met Mr Scuttles.'

Scuttles stepped into the hall. 'Hello, Eddie,' he said.

Scuttles sat on the sofa while Mum took off her coat. Eddie sat opposite him with his knees drawn up under his chin, not knowing what to think.

'So, Eddie, how're you doing?' Scuttles asked, smiling pleasantly. 'Keeping away from that pack of rats, are you?'

Before Eddie could answer – and in fact he had no idea how to respond – Mum answered for him.

'Of course he is, he's learned his lesson, haven't you, love?' Eddie made a grunting sound, but kept his eyes fixed on Scuttles. 'Now then, what about a nice cup of tea?'

Scuttles smiled at Mum then, as she turned to go into the kitchen, he looked back at Eddie. Eddie took a deep breath. He wasn't scared of Scuttles.

Scuttles wasn't wearing his uniform and, with an ordinary jacket and trousers and open-necked shirt, he didn't look half as threatening. No, Eddie definitely wasn't scared of him, but he *was* scared of what he could do, or say.

As if he could tell what Eddie was thinking, Scuttles edged closer to Eddie, until he was sitting on the very edge of the sofa. 'Don't think you'll get away with this afternoon,' he hissed, 'and just consider yourself very lucky I haven't told your mother.'

Eddie jumped up from his chair and stalked into the kitchen. Mum was just waiting for the kettle to boil. She smiled at him and pushed a stray hair out of her eyes. She looked embarrassed. Eddie pushed the door across so that Scuttles couldn't hear.

'What's he doing here?' Eddie demanded.

'He just came for a cup of tea.'

'But why?'

'Just because.'

'Because what?'

'Because I invited him. And, well, he invited me out for dinner.'

'You mean on a *date*?'

'I suppose. Yes.'

'But what about Dad?'

'What about Dad, Eddie? He's gone. And he isn't coming back . . . Oh, Eddie, it's only out for something to eat, it's not the end of the—' She put her arms out and came towards him, but he backed away.

'You can't go out with him, Mum, he's a monster.'

'He's not a monster, Eddie. He just wears a monster's clothes.'

'Well, what's *that* supposed to mean?'

'I mean, he's paid to keep the hospital secure. He has to come on strong. It doesn't mean he's a bad man.'

Eddie looked at her incredulously. Of course Scuttles was a bad man. Everything he had said, everything he had done marked him out as a bad man. What was she thinking of? What on earth was she playing at, to even contemplate going out with a man like Scuttles when his own good father hadn't left home much more than a few days ago?

Eddie could hardly control himself. He pushed past her and pulled the kitchen door open. 'You're bloody mad you are,' he shouted at her, then stomped away along the hall, pausing only to yell in at Scuttles: 'You keep away from my mum, you fat pig!'

Then he opened the front door, stepped out on to the landing, and slammed the door shut behind him.

Eddie was furious.

And suddenly very, very determined.

If he'd had doubts about undertaking his mission before, now nothing on earth was going to give him greater pleasure.

Ten

'Never do anything in a bad temper,' Eddie's dad had once told him, 'you're bound to mess it up.'

Eddie had to admit he'd done *a lot* of things in a bad temper recently, and yes, he had messed them up. He had handed over his trainers, he had attacked Captain Black, he hadn't really given his mum a chance to explain what had gone wrong with her and Dad, preferring to explode at her instead, and now he had stormed out of the apartment in a furious state and determined to take revenge.

Yet he was still determined to take it. He just had to calm down first.

He waited downstairs in the hallway until he saw the lift coming down, then ducked into the shadows as Scuttles left the building. Then he went back up to the apartment and knocked rather sheepishly on the door. Mum opened it, held out her arms to him, and he fell into them. They hugged for several long moments. She messed up his hair and said, 'I know this is difficult for you son, but we're only talking about going out for something to eat. It's not like we're getting married or anything!'

Married! Eddie felt sick. But he didn't say anything. He bit his tongue. Calm. Collected. That was how he was going to be from here on in. He had a mission to undertake. It was no time to get emotional. As his mum hugged him again and began to softly hum a lullaby that had been his favourite when he was a toddler, Eddie began to work out his plan. Mum ruffled his hair again and let him go. She picked up his plate from the window, holding up the sandwich, which was now hard from sitting in the sunlight. 'I don't suppose you'll be wanting this,' she smiled at him. 'What say I make something nice, eh?'

'Aren't you going out for dinner?' Eddie asked.

'Yes of course. But I can still make you something.'

'No, Mum, it's all right. I'll sort myself out.'

She smiled across at him. 'You are a good boy.'

If only she knew, thought Eddie.

At precisely eight o'clock the doorbell rang. Mum shouted from her bedroom. 'Eddie! I'm not ready! Be a love.'

Eddie took a deep breath and went to answer it.

Scuttles was standing there in a grey overcoat with a smart blue suit beneath it. He had combed his hair and smoothed down his moustache and he was grinning widely. He was carrying a bunch of flowers. The grin slipped a little when he saw who it was.

'Good evening, Mr Scuttles,' Eddie said and stepped aside to let him in.

'Good ... evening,' Scuttles said warily, and moved into the hall.

'Mother is not quite ready, may I take your coat, and perhaps get you a drink.'

'Oh,' Scuttles said again, then nodded and slipped off his overcoat. He handed it to Eddie. 'A beer would be good.'

'Coming right up,' Eddie said. 'Please – take a seat.'

Scuttles cleared his throat, nodded, then sat down opposite the TV.

'Only be a little mo!' Mum shouted from her room.

'That's – uh, fine,' Scuttles called back.

Eddie smiled pleasantly at him then carried the overcoat towards his bedroom. 'What sort of beer would you like?' Eddie called back.

'Oh – ah, anything, anything at all,' Scuttles said.

Eddie entered his bedroom, and quickly closed the door behind him. A second later he was going through Scuttles' overcoat pockets – he found a handkerchief, a Mars bar and an electronic pager in the left pocket, and loose change, a mobile phone and a set of car keys in the other. Eddie sighed. It wasn't what he was looking for at all. He held the coat in his hands, momentarily confused – the coat was quite lightweight, but it *felt* heavy. Even with the phone and the change and the other items, it shouldn't be that heavy – he shook the coat and heard a tell-tale jangle. Keys.

Eddie jumped as Scuttles shouted suddenly from the lounge.

'What're you doing with that beer – brewing it?!'

'Just coming!' Eddie called back, then slipped his hand inside the coat, felt around, and located a zip. He pulled it across and reached inside. His fingers closed around a large bunch of keys. He quickly pulled them out, smiled to himself, then threw them under his bed. He lay the coat on top of the bed, then hurried back out of the room and along the hall into the kitchen.

A moment later he appeared in the lounge

doorway. 'Oops,' he said, 'looks like we're all out of beer.'

Scuttles scowled up at him, but before he could speak, Mum appeared behind Eddie.

'All ready!' she announced, smiling across at Scuttles. 'Sorry to keep you.'

'I'll get your coat,' Eddie said, and shot back into his bedroom. When he returned to the lounge Scuttles was complimenting his mother on how well she looked, on how nice her outfit was, on how pleasant her perfume was. Eddie wanted to kick him in the shins. But instead he graciously handed over the overcoat, and wished them a pleasant evening.

'We won't be late,' his mum said as they were going out the door.

'Approximately... what time?' Eddie asked.

'Well, I'm not sure. Why, is there a problem?'

'No... no... just... burglars... you know...'

Mum laughed and messed his hair up again. She would have to stop doing that. It was annoying. And he was twelve. 'Oh, Eddie, burglars, on the seventeenth floor! But don't worry, we'll be back by eleven, okay?'

'Okay.'

'Now, where's my kiss?'

She pursed her lips, expectantly.

Eddie glanced at Scuttles, who was just pulling his overcoat on. Was his brow furrowing? Was he wondering why his coat felt so light? Eddie stepped forward and kissed his mother, then quickly turned and held out his hand to Scuttles. 'Have a good night,' he said, very formally.

Scuttles, surprised, forgot the lightness of his coat, and, somewhat embarrassed, clasped Eddie's hand. 'Why . . . thank you, Eddie,' he said.

Scuttles then shepherded Eddie's Mum out of the front door on to the landing and they both waved goodbye.

Eddie closed the door and leaned against it. He smiled to himself. It was time for action.

He was just crossing towards his bedroom to retrieve the keys when there was a sudden hammering on the front door. When he opened it, Scuttles was standing there. There was no smile this time, his eyes were narrowed and his nostrils flared. 'Forgot my gloves,' he snapped.

Eddie glanced around Scuttles to see his mum standing holding the elevator doors open. Then he looked behind him and saw Scuttles' gloves sitting on the sofa. He darted across, picked them up and hurried back to the door, holding them out before him. But before he could hand them over, Scuttles hissed: 'Don't think I'm fooled by your Mr Nice Guy routine, you little rat. You pull any more smart moves on me, I'll mess up your life badly.' Then he snapped the gloves out of his hand. 'Night then!' Scuttles said jovially, and entirely for Eddie's mum's benefit, as he pulled the door closed behind him.

Eddie stood staring at the door for several moments while his thundering heart calmed down. But his resolve was stronger than ever. 'Watch out, Scuttles,' he said to himself, 'there's a smart move on the way . . .'

Eleven

Eddie entered the Royal Victoria Hospital through a small gate at the very back of the complex which was normally used to deliver catering supplies to the kitchens. He used this gate because he knew from keen observation that although it was covered by a security camera it was rarely checked out by the staff in the security centre on the eighth floor. And it being night time, there were very few people working in the kitchens. So it was easy for Eddie to slip inside and pass through the swing doors which divided the kitchen from the basement storage area. Once hidden in amongst the boxes of tinned foods, Eddie checked his watch. It was now 8.25 pm. Hopefully his mother and Scuttles were sitting happily in a restaurant somewhere far away.

Eddie pulled the baseball cap he was wearing tight down over his eyes, made sure the schoolbag that was weighing heavily on his shoulders was secure, then checked that the coast was clear before darting out from the shelter of the boxes to the base of the stairs that led up to the eighth floor and beyond. He began to climb. It was hard work, but safer than taking the lift, which could stop at any floor and be boarded by security staff. At least on the stairs he could hear people coming up or down.

Eddie climbed as quickly as possible, pausing at each floor to check if the security camera mounted by the doors was blinking on. He had to stop twice, although only for a matter of seconds. He made it to the eighth floor without being detected and within three minutes of setting out. So far, so good.

Before stepping out on to the eighth floor, Eddie peered through the glass panel in the swing doors: the corridor, which was always busy and bustling during the day, was relatively quiet. Of course this floor wasn't entirely taken up by the security offices: there were half a dozen wards, but most of these were devoted to elderly patients who had already settled down for the night. There were nurses on duty, but they had taken up their positions in little clusters, surrounding pots of tea and piles of women's magazines, in alcoves off the main corridor and so were not directly in his line of vision.

Eddie checked again for active cameras, then slipped out from the protection of the swing doors and moved quickly along the corridor towards the security centre which, he was relieved to see, was completely dark. He removed Scuttles' keys and began trying them, one by one. If Bacon or Bap or even Captain Black had been with him, they probably could have told him exactly which key it was, but he was on his own, he had been sent out to prove he could undertake a dangerous mission by himself, without assistance. Eddie tried the fourth key, the fifth, the sixth. He was sweating now. He glanced both ways, he checked the camera. He tried the seventh. The eighth. His fingers were getting slippery. He tried the ninth. The tenth. 'Come on, come on,' he whispered. He tried the eleventh. The twelfth. Then there were voices, and the click, click of nurses' heels from around the corner in the corridor. Come on! He tried the thirteenth, the fourteenth, they were getting closer, closer, any moment they would . . .

The next key slipped effortlessly into the lock. He twisted it quickly, opened the door, slipped inside and clicked it closed behind him. Eddie held his breath as the sound of the heels approached the door, then continued on. Eddie blinked for several moments, getting his bearings. The security centre had slightly tinted windows, allowing the light from outside in the corridor to enter, but it was barely enough to move around by. Still, it was enough for Eddie. He knew what he was looking for.

He crouched down for a moment, catching his breath, reminding himself what Bacon had told him about Scuttles and the security codes. 'Most areas of the hospital we can still get access to with our keys, but certain areas are restricted and entry can only be gained if you know the security codes. Scuttles changes these about once a month, but with Alison Beech visiting on Friday, we're convinced he's going to change them early this month. We need those codes. We need access to all parts of the hospital – with Alison Beech in town there's going to be all sorts of important people around, lots of money, lots of opportunities for us to liberate some of their property, but we really need those codes. We know from hacking into his own surveillance cameras that he keeps them on a computer disk in the second drawer down on his desk. You need to locate them, copy them, and return them so he's none the wiser. Do you understand?'

Eddie had nodded, but then asked: 'How do I copy the disk?'

'That's up to you, Eddie. You're on your own.'

And he was, up on the eighth floor, about to take his revenge on the man who had dared to take his mum out for dinner.

Eddie locked the security centre door behind him, then crossed the outer office, glanced for a moment at the screens which showed the images being recorded by the surveillance cameras, then entered Scuttles' office and closed the door. Now he was in complete darkness. Eddie dropped his schoolbag from his shoulders and reached inside; he felt around and located the small flashlight his mother kept in the kitchen drawer for emergencies. He flicked it on, then moved across the office and knelt down behind Scuttles' desk. He felt for the handle on the second drawer down and pulled – but it was locked.

Eddie tutted. He tried the top drawer, then the third, but they were also locked. He shone his torch on the top of the desk; there was a computer, a half-eaten box of doughnuts, but no sign of any keys. Eddie sighed. He tried forcing the drawer open, but it was too strong for him, and each effort caused too much noise. Eddie thought for a moment, then pulled out the set of keys again and examined them: they were all large door keys, not the kind to open a tiny desk drawer lock. He flicked through them one by one, and then right in the middle of the bunch he found what he was looking for, a tiny key he had missed completely. He smiled to himself and tried it in the lock – it fitted.

Quickly opening the drawer, Eddie shone the light inside. Bingo! Or, *almost* bingo. Instead of the one disk he'd been expecting to find, there were two. Which one had the codes? There was only one way to find out. He placed the disks on top of the table then swung his schoolbag up and removed his laptop from within. It was an old computer, one his dad had bought him to play games on, only to find after a couple of years that it didn't have enough memory to play the new generation of games, so it had sat disused in his bedroom, not good enough to use, but too expensive to throw out. But perfect for copying Scuttles' disk.

Eddie switched the laptop on. He'd checked the battery before coming out, so there was no problem there. In a moment the computer was up and running and he'd slipped the first disk into the slot. Quickly he pulled up a list of Scuttles' files: he ran a finger down them, quietly repeating each title: *Alison Beech, Personnel Files, Financial Projections, Security Codes* – excellent! Eddie copied the last file on to his computer's hard drive, then slipped out the disk and replaced it in the second drawer. Then he placed the second disk into the laptop and opened it. There was only one file on it – and it was labelled *Reservoir Pups*!

Scuttles kept a file on the gang! Perfect – Eddie would not only be stealing the security codes, he'd also be able to find out exactly what Scuttles had on the gang. They'd think he was a real hero! Eddie began to copy the file – then froze. Somebody was unlocking the Security Centre door.

Twelve

Eddie had about three seconds to throw himself under the desk before the door to Scuttles' inner office opened and the light went on. Eddie, his knees drawn up against his face, didn't dare breathe; he kept his eyes tight shut as if in some way that would prevent anyone from seeing him. *Please, please, please, please, please, please,* he kept saying, over and over to himself. He heard someone *tut* and then cross the office floor towards him.

He squeezed himself into an even tighter ball as the person stopped at the foot of the desk, then tutted again and a voice he vaguely recognised said, 'Lazy bugger.' He heard something close, something open, and then the whole desk vibrated as one of the drawers of the desk was slammed shut. Eddie almost let out a shout of fright. He bit down hard on his lip to stop himself. There was a jangle of keys – the keys he had stolen from Scuttles – and the sound of a lock turning. Eddie opened his eyes a frightened fraction and saw two large snakeskin cowboy boots. A moment later they suddenly moved away from the desk and back across the office to the open door. The light was just being switched off when the Cowboy said, 'I have them.'

Then the door closed.

As he slowly uncurled from his ball beneath the desk, Eddie heard chairs being pulled out and men talking in the outer office.

He let out a huge pent-up breath, and sucked greedily at the air around him. He had had a reprieve, but he was anything but safe. He was trapped in Scuttles' private office.

Eddie put his head in his hands and tried to think.

What was he even doing here, undertaking a stupid mission for a stupid gang? How stupid was he?

And what was he going to do? Remain under the desk until they left? They could be there all night.

He glanced at the illuminated dial of his watch – it was almost nine o'clock. He had two hours to think of some way of getting out of Scuttles' office without getting caught, and then make it home before his mum. If she arrived home and he wasn't there – well, she'd be on to the police right away.

What a disaster!

He rubbed his brow.

What to do, what to do, what to do, what to do.

The easiest thing was to stay where he was, wait them out, even if they were there all night. He would make something up to satisfy his mum – he'd been sleepwalking, he'd been out at a friend's house and fallen asleep, he'd set off to try and find his dad . . . yeah, maybe she would go for that one. Maybe.

But . . .

. . . what if the other security guards stayed there all night, waiting to be relieved by Scuttles? He'd come straight into his office in the morning and find him.

. . . or he might even come into the office after his dinner with Mum. Maybe he did that every night, maybe he couldn't sleep until he was satisfied everything was safe and well at the hospital.

Eddie knew he couldn't take that chance.

He had to do something.

Eddie crept cautiously out from beneath the desk. Even though there were no windows in this inner office, he didn't dare switch his flashlight back on. He got on to his knees and felt up on to the top of the desk, planning to retrieve his lap-top. But it wasn't there. With a sickening feeling Eddie realised what had happened, that the Cowboy had found the computer switched on and guessed it was Scuttles. So he'd closed it and put it away in the second drawer which was – he pulled at it – locked. And Cowboy had taken the keys with him.

This was going from bad to worse.

Eddie stood and padded across to the door. He knelt down beside it and applied his eye to the keyhole. He needed to know just how bad his situation was, if the men in the outer office looked like they were planning to be there for a while. He already knew, more or less, because he could smell coffee and yes – doughnuts. They were probably the late shift, and with nothing going on in the rest of the hospital, they planned to put their feet up until morning.

By moving his head to different angles against the keyhole, Eddie was able to get a pretty good view of the outer office. He could see Cowboy sitting with his boots up on his desk. Opposite him there were two men he hadn't seen before, neither of them wearing the Hospital Security uniform. One of them, a bald man wearing round glasses, was sitting looking at a computer screen, and making notes in a small notebook. The other was a big, muscular looking guy with a goatee beard. He was peering down at what the bald guy was writing.

Eddie could barely make out what they were saying, just managing to get little snatches of it.

'You're sure . . . the right . . . codes,' the bald man was saying.

'Yeah, yeah, yeah . . .' Cowboy was saying. 'Alison Beech . . .'

'We have the weapons . . .' the big muscular guy was saying.

'. . . biggest kidnap in . . .' the bald man was saying.

'. . . thank Scuttles for everything . . .' Cowboy was saying.

And then the voices grew more indistinct for several moments. Eddie pressed his ear against the keyhole, not quite understanding what he'd been hearing, but certain that it wasn't good.

That men who should have been talking about football, or girls, or their work, were instead talking about security codes, weapons and kidnapping Alison Beech.

Thirteen

For the next hour, the men in the outer office sat hunched over what seemed to Eddie to be a map, or perhaps a plan of the hospital. Their voices dropped even lower until he could barely make anything out at all, except when they suddenly burst into laughter or clapped their hands together and shouted, 'Yeah, good one!'

Then the phone rang in the outer office and the Cowboy lifted it. 'Mr Scuttles,' the Cowboy said. He paused, then said: 'Everything's under control. Don't worry about it. Relax, you deserve it after all the work you've put in. It's quite a plan.' Then he laughed again. 'Is she a good kisser, then?' the Cowboy asked, then laughed again at Scuttles' response.

They were talking about his mum. Eddie wanted to go out there and punch the Cowboy. Scuttles too. Not content with taking up arms and kidnapping Ireland's and perhaps the world's richest woman, Scuttles and his gang were now making fun of his mother, laughing about secret, intimate things, which in Eddie's mind was just as big a crime. *He* could laugh about his mother's secret, intimate things, nobody else could. Scuttles by name, Scuttles by nature – he was like a huge black beetle that crawled about the kitchen floor.

After Cowboy put the phone down, the bald guy and the muscular guy stood up and shook hands with him, then slipped out of the room. Eddie had his fingers crossed that Cowboy would go with them, but instead he put his feet back up on his desk and switched on a small radio. Country and western music drifted through the security centre.

Eddie had to do something *now*.

Perhaps if he just pulled open the door and ran for it, got past Cowboy before he had a chance to move? Sure, he'd know who Eddie was, but at least he'd get the chance to alert the world to their plan to kidnap Alison Beech.

Alternatively, Cowboy might catch him, and kill him.

And then it struck him – the phone. Cowboy was on duty, he was obliged to investigate any security alerts at the hospital.

Eddie cautiously made his way back to the desk. He took out his flashlight, but lessened the risk slightly by cupping his hands around the beam.

He shone it down on Scuttles' phone – good, there was an extension number for the outer office. Eddie quickly rehearsed what he was going to say, then lifted the receiver and pressed the number. A moment later the Cowboy's phone began to ring. Cowboy tutted, lifted his feet down off his desk, and answered it. 'Security,' he said bluntly.

Eddie deepened his voice as much as he could. 'Security – this is Geoff down in the laundry, I think we might have an intruder down here.'

'An intruder. Okay, Geoff, I—'

Eddie carefully replaced the receiver, then hurried across to the door. He bent back down to the keyhole in time to see Cowboy pull on his jacket. It was working. Eddie felt a sudden rush of adrenalin. He'd outfoxed him. Cowboy opened the door of the Security Centre and hurried away down the corridor. A moment later Eddie stepped out of the same door, smiled after the Cowboy's retreating figure and was about to turn in the opposite direction when the Cowboy stopped suddenly, patted his pocket and said: 'Keys.'

The Cowboy spun on his heel back towards the office, but for the first few steps didn't look up, didn't see Eddie frozen in the doorway.

But then, of course, he did.

'Hey!' the Cowboy shouted.

Eddie wasn't about to stop for a chat.

He took off.

He charged along the corridor, smashing through the double doors at the end of it, then turned left along another corridor.

'Stop!' the Cowboy yelled, the metallic heels of his boots clicking madly as he thundered after him. As he ran the Cowboy lifted his walkie-talkie – then thought better of it. *What if the boy had heard . . .*

Eddie had maybe a twenty metre start on him. He made the stairs and began to take them three, four and five at a time, using a handrail to launch himself forward. Behind him he heard the swing doors crash again and the Cowboy's urgent feet on the steps.

Eddie was sure he could outrun the Cowboy – and the Cowboy seemed to know it too, because he suddenly had second thoughts about calling in support. He'd catch the boy first, worry about the consequences later. He pulled out his walkie-talkie again and barked: 'I'm in pursuit of an intruder, I'm on the stairs between levels seven and six! I want all exits sealed – do you understand? All exits sealed!'

Eddie heard him clearly. He'd been heading for the kitchens where he'd entered before, but now he couldn't chance it – whatever security guards were on duty in the hospital would be converging on that very area. He also had to get off the stairs.

When he reached the third floor Eddie burst through on to the ward corridor – the maternity wing, mothers and babies. He charged towards a set of automatic doors – then cursed to himself as they failed to open. He glanced to one side, and realised that this was one of the areas in the hospital that required a security code to enter. The Cowboy appeared at the far end of the corridor. 'You! Stop!' he yelled, and somewhere beyond the unyielding doors a dozen babies began to cry.

'Hey – what's your game?' a nurse suddenly bellowed at him.

She was right in his face. She made a grab for him, but he managed to duck down out of her reach. He raced half a dozen metres back towards the Cowboy then turned abruptly left into a side corridor. At the far end of it he could see a lift, not one that was normally used for patients, but a small one, for staff only. He raced towards it and pressed the button. Cowboy skidded around the corner and began to thunder towards him. Eddie didn't think he had time to wait for the lift – he turned right, but the corridor finished there in a dead end. He turned left – and saw another security guard hurrying towards him.

He was trapped.

But just for a moment.

The lift doors opened behind him and he turned and leapt in, hitting the button for the basement and almost in the same motion jabbing a lower button which would automatically close the lift doors.

In reality he only had to wait a couple of heartbeats for the doors to close, but they were long, slow heartbeats during which the only thing that seemed to be moving fast was the Cowboy bearing down on the elevator.

He was getting closer and closer and closer and closer and the doors were moving slower and slower and slower . . . and then suddenly they were shut. The Cowboy, in his frustration, hammered on the closed doors with his fists. If he'd been using his wits he could have merely pressed the lift button again and the doors would have opened. But he didn't, and by then it was too late – Eddie was away.

* * *

Eddie held his breath as the elevator doors opened on to the clank and grind of the basement – but there was nobody waiting. He stepped out into a dark and forbidding place. Down here, where the furnaces boiled day and night to heat the hospital and burn the filthy sheets and disease-ridden bandages, where the laundries vibrated and spun like dozens of little earthquakes, and most of all, where the dead were stored, cold and hard, waiting to be claimed by their relatives. It was a world that existed in a weird half-light, which was fine for Eddie. But it was the smell that got him. It was like there was a battle going on between good and evil, the antiseptic odour of the hospital and the poisoned stench of death and disease. It made him feel quite dizzy. And then, in the distance, he heard the rapid beat of feet hurrying along deserted corridors. They were coming for him.

Eddie steadied himself against the wall for a moment, desperately trying to remember the layout of this basement area, if there were any exits that might not be immediately covered by the Cowboy's security team, any hiding places were he was unlikely to be discovered.

C'mon, Eddie, make your mind up! The footsteps

were getting louder, they were coming from several different directions. *C'mon!*

Eddie turned to his left, ran half a dozen metres, then tried a door. Locked. He tried a second. Locked. A third – it opened, but there was a light already on and he hesitated for moment – but then the footsteps were suddenly so near, so close to changing from a noise to a physical shape, just about to round the corner and catch him, that he knew he had no choice. Eddie slipped inside, then carefully, carefully closed the door behind him. A moment later the footsteps passed the door, continued on for a little bit, then stopped. He heard voices, but couldn't make out what they were saying. Then, further along the corridor, doors began to open and close. They were searching for him, room by room.

Eddie looked at his new surroundings for the first time – and shuddered. Six long tables lay in front of him, and on each one a white sheet covering something beneath. The room was cold, deliberately cold, because they had to keep the dead bodies cold to stop them rotting too soon. This was where they brought people who had died on the operating table, bodies to be cleaned up, to have their blood drained and their bits and pieces sewn back up so that they wouldn't drip and ooze. Of all the places he had been in the hospital, this had the strongest smell of antiseptic – they must have sprayed, and sprayed and sprayed – yet nothing could cover up the worst smell of all – death.

And at that moment, behind a small door on the other side of the room, a toilet flushed.

Without thinking – because if he had thought about it, he wouldn't have done it in a million years – Eddie dashed across the room, pulled up one of the sheets and slipped under it.

He lay beside an old, dead, naked woman with his eyes tight shut. But he could feel cold hard flesh against his cheek. He lay as still as the body beside him as someone emerged from a toilet, humming a tune Eddie remembered his mum singing around the house: 'If You Like My Body, and You Think I'm Sexy'. Eddie opened his eyes again. The sheet was thin enough for him to be able to see shapes through it, and he could now see the outline of a large man with something in his hand; Eddie heard the swirl of water in a bucket, and then a sponge being dunked in it. A sheet was pulled from a body on the next table to his and the man began to wash it, pausing only to light a cigarette and jam it in his mouth.

Eddie lay there for five minutes, cold, frightened and miserable, as the man completed washing the body down.

And then he came and stood over Eddie.

'Now then,' the man said, 'who's next for a nice little bath?'

Fourteen

There comes a point in your life when things cannot possibly get any worse, when they can only get better. Eddie, who had lost his father, his home, and his friends, who had attacked a disabled boy, been seized twice by Scuttles, been kidnapped by the Reservoir Pups, who had been turned into a thief and burglar; Eddie, who was now lying beside a naked dead old woman, and about to be discovered by a man who washed corpses for a living, was at that point in his life. Things really could not get any worse, what he needed and prayed for was a stroke of good luck.

Not one minute from now, not one week from now, but *right now*.

And it came with a knock on the door, and a grunt from the body-washer, who hesitated even as his fat fingers curled around the edge of the sheet, then tutted and let go of it and turned away.

Eddie's heart felt like it was going to explode. He heard the door open, and then the Cowboy's voice: 'We're looking for a kid. Have you seen a kid?'

'A live kid?' the body-washer said.

'Yes, of course, a live kid. Have you seen a kid?'

'Nope,' the body-washer said, 'ain't no-one here but me and the stiffs. Who're you after?'

'Doesn't matter,' Cowboy said, then turned and walked away.

The body-washer watched him go for a moment, then said: 'Please yourself,' after him, and closed the door. He crossed back to Eddie's table.

Eddie's good luck lasted precisely thirty seconds.

Then the body-washer said: 'You can come out now, kid.'

Eddie wasn't sure what he was hearing. Was the body-washer talking to him? Who else? But he remained frozen where he was until slowly the sheet was peeled back from him. Eddie stared wide-eyed up at the large, red-faced man looking down at him.

'Uh,' Eddie said. And then added, 'There's a perfectly good explanation for this.'

The body-washer held up his hands. 'Don't want to hear it, kid, don't want to know. All I know is if those guys are after you, you must be doing something right. Now unless you've grown really close to that old granny, I'd get down from there.'

Eddie didn't need a second invitation. He

jumped down from the table, then glanced back at the corpse. He shivered. He hugged himself and looked helplessly at the body-washer, who laughed and replaced the sheet over the corpse. 'Don't you worry about this old dear,' he said, 'she's happy somewhere else, she's not hanging around here. She's just a husk, like an old empty coconut.'

Eddie nodded, then cautiously ventured: 'Are you going to . . . ?'

'What? Call back those Nazis? Turn you in?' Eddie nodded. The body-washer shook his head. 'I don't know who you are, and I don't know what you've done, but if you've got one over on the likes of them, then fair play to you.'

'But . . . why?' Eddie asked.

'Because every morning I park my bike outside here, like I have every right to do, and every morning that idiot comes and makes me move it away because I don't have the right sticker on it. Is it my fault this hospital is so disorganised they can't get me the right sticker? *He* knows I have the right to park out there, *I* know I have the right to park out there, but does that make any difference? No, it does not. So, anything that annoys him is okay by me. Him and his stupid damn cowboy boots – who does he think he is?'

Eddie smiled for the first time that night. 'Well, I uh . . . well, thank you. How did you know I was even here?'

'Because when you've been in here for as long as I have, believe you me, you can hear the slightest breath. Now then – I suppose you'll be wanting a way out of here, some way they're not going to catch you.'

Eddie nodded hopefully.

The body-washer signalled for Eddie to follow him and then led him to what looked like a small set of cupboard doors on the far side of the room. He opened them and showed Eddie what appeared to be a narrow tunnel leading away into darkness. Eddie looked at it warily.

'Where does it go?' he asked.

'Outside,' said the body-washer. 'We don't like to take the dead bodies away through the hospital where the patients might see them. So the undertakers drive up to this chute, they send the coffin down, we fill it up and send it back up. It's all electric of course, but it's quite noisy, so if you don't mind I won't turn it on. Just scurry up there, open the doors at the other end, and you'll be outside the building. After that, it's up to you.'

Eddie looked at the tunnel, and then at the body-washer. 'Thanks,' he said. He glanced back at the room full of bodies, then pulled himself through the doors. But before he could set off, the body-washer reached over and touched Eddie's shoulder. It made him jump, and for a moment he feared it had all been a joke, that really the body-washer was intending to trap him in the tunnel until he could summon the Cowboy back. But when Eddie looked back the body-washer merely extended his hand and said, 'I'm Barney.'

Eddie reached back and shook Barney's hand. 'I'm Eddie.'

Barney smiled. 'Good luck, Eddie,' he said, and then, quite sadly, Eddie later thought, 'Any time you want to visit, feel free. Gets kind of quiet down here.'

Eddie smiled again, nodded, then turned back into the tunnel.

Fifteen

Eddie arrived home exactly seventeen seconds before his mum and Scuttles.

He ran like the wind, hit the elevator, let himself into the apartment, guzzled down a pint of water without stopping for breath, heard a key in the door, then giggling from the hall. As nonchalantly as possible, Eddie wandered out of the kitchen, just as Scuttles was moving in to kiss his mother.

Eddie coughed.

His mum backed quickly away, looking embarrassed. Scuttles looked daggers at Eddie.

'Oh, Eddie!' his mum exclaimed, 'I thought you'd be in bed ages ago.'

'I couldn't sleep,' Eddie said.

'Hope you weren't worrying about me!' his mum said with a little too much enthusiasm. 'You don't mind if Bernie comes in for a drink, do you?'

Eddie glared across at Scuttles. This man, a man who was planning a kidnapping, who had threatened and harassed Eddie ever since he'd arrived in the city, was looking for an invitation to stay. He would probably attempt to kiss her again. He would probably try and sleep in the same bed as her. Oh, if only she knew, if only. He had to get Scuttles out.

'I think I'm going to be sick,' Eddie said, suddenly clutching his stomach. 'I think I'm going to throw up.'

He made a kind of a gagging sound.

'Oh darling,' his mum said, glancing apologetically at Scuttles as she moved towards her son, 'what's wrong? Have you eaten something? Are you . . .' and she put a hand to his brow which was sticky with the effort of running home at a hundred miles an hour. 'Oh dear, he *does* have a temperature.'

Scuttles cleared his throat. 'Maybe if he got a cold drink. Went back to bed.'

Eddie groaned. He started to cough. His mum hugged him. 'I need to see to him,' she said.

Scuttles blew air out of his cheeks. 'Well,' he said, 'maybe I should go.'

Eddie's mum nodded. 'I just worry about him. You understand, don't you?'

'Sure I do,' Scuttles said, though he didn't look to Eddie like he understood. Or perhaps he understood too much. 'I'll see you tomorrow then,

Lianne,' he said, then gave her a wink. 'Big day'n all.'

He turned to the door and opened it.

'Oh Bernie – wait,' Eddie's mum said, and as he hesitated, she hurried up to him and kissed him on the lips. 'Thanks for a lovely evening.'

Eddie really did feel ill this time. He wanted to jump on Scuttles' back and pull his ears off.

Mum closed the door after him, then turned back towards Eddie, smiling – a smile that quickly slipped when she saw the thunderous look on his face.

'Why did you do that?' Eddie snapped.

'Do what?'

'What do you think! Kiss him!'

'Because I wanted to, Eddie.'

'But . . . but . . . but what about Dad?'

'What about Dad? He's gone.'

'He's not gone! He's just . . . away. And why *him*? Why Scuttles? You don't know what he's like.'

'No, Eddie – *you* don't know what he's like. He's actually quite lovely.' And she looked all dreamy for a moment.

Eddie snapped her out of it. 'He is not!' he shouted. 'He's a . . . a kidnapper!' There – he'd said it. 'I know all about him, Mum.'

'Eddie – what *are* you talking about?'

'He's part of a gang! They're going to kidnap Alison Beech. They're going to kidnap her tomorrow! Mum! We have to call the police, we have to—'

'Eddie! Calm down!'

'I can't calm down, they're going to—'

'EDDIE!'

Eddie tried his best. 'Mum . . . please listen to me, he's going to—'

But she held up her hand to stop him. 'Oh, Eddie. Why can't you be happy for me, that I've met someone? Instead of making up your silly stories, why don't you think about me for once?'

'I *am* thinking about you! They have a plan, I heard them, I was at the hospital tonight! The Cowboy, a couple of others! They chased me! I had to hide with the dead bodies! Mum, you have to believe me! You have to call the police.'

'If I call anyone, Eddie, I'm going to call the doctor, because your fever is obviously worse than I thought. Now, I want you to go to bed and I'll come in in a moment with a nice drink of water, and I'll take your temperature.'

'Mum!'

'Go! It's late and I have a big day tomorrow!'

'I know! Alison Beech! They're going to kidnap her.'

'Well, then they're going to have to kidnap me as well, because I've won the lottery and I'm showing her round the hospital.' She gave Eddie a triumphant smile. 'Now, get to bed, Eddie, it's very late. And I don't think we'll really be needing the doctor, will we?'

The problem was, Eddie was exactly like his mother, and she was exactly like him. The more he was told not to do something, the more likely he was to do it. And the more Eddie implored his mother to call the police, or at the very least call into work sick so she wouldn't run the risk of getting injured or kidnapped, the more angry and determined she became.

'Life's fickle lottery,' she said dreamily, clutching her bosom, 'has chosen me to meet and greet and guide the incredible Alison Beech.' And then her voice took on a much tougher hue. 'And *you* aren't going to spoil my big day. I had enough of that from your father.'

So Eddie went to bed. He could hardly sleep because his mind was racing – about the kidnap plot, his laptop locked in Scuttles' desk, about his mother kissing Scuttles. When he finally did drift off for a few minutes he found himself back under the cold, white sheet with the cold, white body of somebody's old grandmother and that forced him back awake again, bathed in sweat and his heart pounding.

So he tossed and turned and cursed, until finally his thoughts converged on the only possible solution to his many problems. The Reservoir Pups.

Sixteen

Eddie was up shortly after dawn – but not early enough to beat his mother. She was immersing herself in as many Alison Beech lotions and potions as she could manage for her big day. Eddie stood in the bathroom doorway as she relaxed beneath the Alison Beech Aromatherapy bath foam – 'pure essential oils of lavender, ylang ylang and patchouli relax your senses and soften your skin with Alison Beech's anti-stress bath foam' – and said, 'I'm going out for a ride on my bike. Maybe that's what's wrong with me, I need some fresh air.'

Mum smiled at him and said, 'Be careful of the traffic.' As he backed out she said: 'Wish me luck on my big day.'

'Good luck.'

'Thank you. And Eddie?'

'What?'

'Bernie. Mr Scuttles. He's not such an ogre when you get to know him.'

Eddie didn't reply. He took his bike down in the lift, then cycled out of the nurses' quarters and across to the edge of the Rivers. While traffic was already building up on the motorway, everything was quiet at the entrance to the sprawling housing estate. Eddie knew it was because very few of the people who lived there had jobs to go to. He rode forward through the estate, losing himself several times in the tight and winding streets before he found himself outside the Reservoir Pups headquarters at a little before seven o'clock. It was ridiculous to expect to find even the most conscientious street bandit up and about this early in the morning, but he had no alternative.

Eddie rapped on the door. It sprang open without a moment's delay and Bacon peered out, looked left, right, then signalled for Eddie to enter.

'I need to speak to Captain—' Eddie began, but Bacon cut him off.

'Hurry up, we've been expecting you.'

Eddie pushed his bike through the door, and followed Bacon down a corridor which twisted and turned its way through the several houses which had been knocked together to form the Pups HQ.

'I didn't know if there'd be anyone here,' Eddie said to Bacon's back.

'There's always someone here,' Bacon replied,

without looking back. 'We're a twenty-four hour operation.'

The place was indeed a hive of activity, the corridors and stairs teeming with kids running busily back and forth. Each room he passed was as busy as it had been on his first visit.

'I went to the hospital,' Eddie began to explain, 'you won't believe what—'

'Save it for the Captain.'

Eddie nodded. Bacon led him on to the bottom of the corridor, then stopped at the entrance to a room different to the one in which he'd previously met Captain Black. The boy with the crew cut hair he'd last seen in the hospital car park was standing outside it, arms folded. 'You can leave your bike with Sean.' Eddie nodded at Sean and then tentatively held out the bike to him. Sean immediately took hold of it by the handlebars and wheeled it away, without a word, or any indication indeed that Eddie even existed.

Eddie was beginning to wonder just how big the Pups' headquarters really was. Bacon led him into a room which was much larger than any of the others – in fact it was big enough to be called a hall. There was a small wooden platform like a stage at one end of it. Bacon reached up and hit a button by the door, and immediately three loud alarms sounded, one after the other. Boys and girls began to appear from everywhere, dozens and dozens thundering down corridors and appearing through other previously hidden doors to assemble in several tight lines of military formation across the floor of the hall. Some even came sliding down on ropes from rooms secreted in the ceiling. Eddie was astounded, hugely impressed and quite a bit apprehensive.

Captain Black then appeared at the back of the hall, rolling down a small ramp on to the stage.

Eddie jumped suddenly as Bacon shouted from behind him: 'Reservoir Pups – on parade!'

There was an immediate clicking of feet as the assembled gang stood to attention, and Eddie found himself joining in.

Captain Black nodded at his gang. 'We have a prospective new member.' Eddie felt all eyes turn on him. 'His name is Eddie Malone and he's not from the Rivers.'

This didn't go down well. The gang members muttered unhappily amongst themselves and peered more closely at him.

'This doesn't mean that he is entirely without merit – he's only been in the city for a week, and he's already been arrested twice by Scuttles.'

This received much more approval. Eddie smiled awkwardly.

'As you are aware – and as you have all successfully undertaken yourselves – each man, or woman, who wishes to join our ranks must complete a dangerous task. Eddie's mission was to retrieve the new security codes from Scuttles' headquarters.' Captain Black now gave Eddie his full attention. 'Eddie Malone – will you step forward now and present the codes.'

Eddie could feel every eye in the hall burning into him as he took one step closer to the stage. He broke into a cold sweat.

'I . . . I . . . don't have them,' he stammered.

A displeased murmur came from behind.

Captain Black glared down at him. 'Then why are you even here?'

'Because I came to warn you . . . to ask for your help. My mum . . . I mean . . . I went to the hospital, I broke in like you said . . .'

'Do you have the codes?'

'No! I mean – I got them, but then the Cowboy—'

'Do you have the codes?'

'I *had* them! But then I got trapped and couldn't get them out . . .'

'*Very* disappointing,' Captain Black said, shaking his head sadly. Then he suddenly snapped his fingers. 'Get him out of here.'

Eddie was immediately grabbed by three gang members. They began to drag him backwards.

Eddie strained against them, and managed to stand his ground for a moment, long enough for him to shout: 'You don't understand! Scuttles is going to kidnap Alison Beech! Today! At the hospital! You have to help!'

'I *understand*, Eddie Malone,' Captain Black said, his voice low and threatening, 'that you have failed in your mission and are no longer welcome in our headquarters. And if you divulge anything that you have learned about us, you will be severely punished. Now, please *remove him*.'

Eddie, the hisses and boos of gang members echoing in his ears, was dragged out of the hall, then back along the winding corridor. Bacon was already waiting at the front door, which was open.

'Please,' Eddie began to say to him, 'you have to believe me . . .'

But Bacon didn't have to do anything. He grabbed Eddie by his jumper, pulling him out of the hands of his captors, and hurled him out on to the street.

Eddie landed hard on his stomach. He let out a yelp of pain then rolled over to see Bacon standing in the doorway.

'I knew you were a waste of time,' he sneered. He was about to step back inside, then hesitated and snapped back at Eddie, 'And we're keeping your bike.'

A moment later the front door of the headquarters of the Reservoir Pups was slammed shut.

Seventeen

Eddie limped through the deserted Rivers estate, his eyes darting about, waiting to be attacked and beaten or robbed and further humiliated. He had come as a friend and comrade, seeking help, and was now retreating home as a battered and defeated enemy without a friend in the world. Oh, sorry, one friend: a man who washed dead bodies for a living. Great – if that was all he could claim for twelve years of existence on Planet Earth, then he really wasn't doing very well at all.

By the time he got home, his mother had already left for work. There was a note from her pinned to the fridge.

It said: *(1) Have a nice day. (2) Hope you're feeling better. (3) Don't go near the hospital today. (4) Please don't go near the hospital today. (5) I mean it.*

Eddie sighed, went to the window, and gazed out first over the Rivers, then the motorway, then finally allowed his eyes to settle on the hospital itself. Although the main gates were open, two of Scuttles' security team were standing guard, stopping drivers and checking they had invitations. Ambulances came and went as normal, but there were fewer patients; appointments had been cancelled, those who were very nearly better had been sent home. This was to be a special day for the hospital, it didn't want to spoil things by having a lot of sick people wandering around. After all, Alison Beech was all about health and fitness, that's why she was giving money to the hospital, to make people better.

Eddie drummed his fingers against the window. Soon, very soon, Alison Beech would arrive full of good intentions but find herself caught up in a violent incident that would probably result in her kidnapping. And what about those who tried to stop it – what about his mother? She was such an ardent fan of Alison Beech that it wasn't beyond the bounds of possibility that she might hurl herself in front of the kidnappers, that she might take a bullet to save Alison Beech's life.

And he was supposed to sit there and watch TV?

Eddie hurried back out, down the elevator and across the small area of waste ground which led around the back of the hospital. There were several gates here, but each one was manned by a security guard. This wasn't a problem. He knew the area like the back of his hand by now, and within a few minutes he'd slipped over the wall at an unguarded section and ducked down amongst the vehicles in the car park. He wasn't absolutely certain what he was planning to do, but he knew he needed to get into the hospital, get close to his mother and protect her at all costs.

At least there was no sign of the Reservoir Pups. They probably knew better than to try pulling any of their scams on a day when security was so tight. Eddie moved quickly along the rows of cars until he was within sight of the main entrance to the hospital. This was richly festooned with hanging baskets of flowers and banners proclaiming 'Welcome Alison Beech' and 'Alison Beech, Saving Our Hospitals'. There was a large group of people standing waiting for her to arrive: Eddie could see Scuttles, in a smart new uniform, a man with a chunky gold chain around his neck he presumed was the Lord Mayor of the city, half a dozen important-looking men in impressive suits, a similar number of ladies in their Sunday best and, in amongst them, in a freshly pressed, crisp, blue nurse's uniform, his mother. Standing off to one side there was a number of press photographers, camera crews and reporters. As he watched, this press pack suddenly surged forwards towards a long white stretch limousine which was just purring to a stop, escorted on either side by police officers on motorbikes. Scuttles immediately scuttled forward to open one of the rear doors, and a moment later possibly the most beautiful, radiant woman Eddie had ever seen stepped out.

Alison Beech.

She looked like an angel. Her hair was long and blonde, and when she smiled it was as if someone had switched on the Christmas lights. She dazzled everyone around her.

She posed benevolently for the cameras, then allowed the Mayor to kiss her hand. Eddie could see his mother with her fingers nervously touching her lips. One of the men in suits then ushered Alison Beech towards the hospital. Patients and nurses alike applauded as she entered the building.

Eddie's view of Alison Beech's progress into the hospital was blocked for a moment as a large white van slowly cruised past. With a shudder Eddie recognised the driver – the bald man he had overheard plotting in the security centre. A sign on the side of the van read *Braxton Hicks Contractors*. The van increased its speed again and disappeared around the corner of the main building. Eddie took one last look back towards the hospital entrance, at the limo, at the police escort, at the group surrounding Alison Beech as she made her regal way into the hospital – then darted after the van.

He found it parked with its engine running on double yellow lines at the rear of the main building. The van's bodywork was speckled with rust, its rear windows were thick with dirt and the number plate was cracked. Eddie pressed himself into a doorway and watched as the side door opened and the bald man and his well-muscled friend emerged. Each was carrying a holdall and wearing the kind of blue boiler suits which the maintenance men wore around the hospital. They looked both ways, then hurried towards the closest entrance. The bald man reached up and keyed in the security code. Immediately the door opened inwards, and they entered the hospital.

Eddie glanced back at the van. There was a pale elbow just visible, resting on the driver's open window. So he couldn't just dart after them or he'd be seen – not that he had the code that would allow him to enter. What should he do? He could try and damage what was clearly the getaway vehicle –

but what good would that do if his mother was already dead or injured trying to protect Alison Beech? He had to somehow prevent the kidnapping taking place. He had to get inside. Eddie peered along the wall – and saw a bike resting beside the entrance to Barney's tunnel. That was his way in – the way the dead bodies came out. Now it was just a question of getting there without being spotted. He looked back to the van – and was astonished to see Bacon and Bap standing beside it, chatting to the driver. *My God*, Eddie thought, his heart sinking even further, *are they part of it as well? Is that why I was sent to get the codes, because the Reservoir Pups were involved in the kidnap plot?* But then the driver's door opened suddenly and a man with a ponytail jumped out and started to chase Bacon and Bap away up the street. He kicked out, catching Bacon on the bum. Bacon yelped but didn't stop. Eddie breathed a sigh of relief – they were just pulling another scam.

While the pony-tailed man gave chase, shouting and cursing after the Pups, Eddie darted along the side of the building then scrambled through the swing doors into the tunnel. He crawled quickly along it and emerged cautiously on the other side. Barney was standing on the far side of the room washing a body. He didn't look at all surprised when Eddie appeared, he merely glanced up, sponge in hand and said: 'Hiya, Eddie. What's up?'

'Someone's trying to kidnap Alison Beech.'

Barney blinked at him for a moment. Then he nodded and said: 'Do you want to help me wash the bodies?'

'No, Barney. No thanks. Not today.' He began to cross the room. 'I . . . just wanted to say hello.'

Barney nodded. 'Well. That's nice.' He returned his attention to the body he was cleaning. 'That's nice,' he said again.

Eddie slipped out of the room and then dashed along the corridor – just in time to see Baldy and Muscles enter an elevator. Eddie held back until the doors were closed then rushed forward and watched to see which floor they were heading for. First . . . second . . . third . . . fourth . . . the fourth. Then that's where they were planning it. Now – where was Alison Beech? Which part of the hospital had she reached on her grand tour? Certainly not the fourth – he had time, he still had time.

Eddie charged along the corridor, pushed through a set of swing doors and then began to take the stairs to the first floor three at a time. He didn't even care if the security cameras were watching him now. He had to protect his mother. He emerged on the first floor and stared down the long corridor – no sign of them. Eddie hit the stairs again and raced to the second floor. Breathing hard, he burst through the doors just in time to see Alison Beech step into an elevator at the far end, quickly followed by as many of her adoring audience as could squeeze in. Eddie spun on his heels and thundered up the stairs to the third.

It was now or never.

As Alison Beech emerged from the elevator, with his mum right beside her, pointing this way and that, Eddie stood at the far end, quickly studying the fire alarm on the wall. It was a small red glass-fronted box, with a notice pinned above it which read: *Break in case of fire*. Chance or fate had brought him to this fire alarm. He would smash it, the alarm would cause enough panic to frighten off the kidnappers and the day would be saved.

Eddie smashed the glass.

Or, at least, he tried to.

He punched it, but succeeded only in bruising his knuckles.

He tried again and again.

He tried his elbow.

He tried his forehead.

The glass would not break.

Then he found a small metal fire extinguisher attached to the opposite wall. Hard enough to break the glass, light enough to wield. He stepped across, pulled it out of its bracket, then dragged it back with both hands, ready to smash the glass.

Except that as he pulled it back his arm was suddenly clutched by one huge hand, and a very angry voice said, 'You little *rat*.'

Eighteen

Eddie stared, distraught, into Scuttles' huge, angry eyes as the fire extinguisher clattered to the floor.

'Eddie?' He turned his face slightly to see his mum, Alison Beech, the Lord Mayor and a dozen other dignitaries hurrying down the corridor towards them.

Scuttles, pinning Eddie to the wall with one giant hand, shouted back at the onrushing global superstar, 'Don't worry, ma'am, all under control here! Just one of the local gutter rats trying to spoil your day!' Then he turned back to Eddie and hissed: 'You've really done it this time, rat-boy! I found your computer! You stole my security codes! You and your bloody gang are going to—!'

But Eddie suddenly cut in, screaming up the corridor: 'He's trying to kidnap you! He's trying to kidnap you!'

Scuttles' mouth dropped open. 'I'm trying to *what*?'

'He's trying to—' and then Eddie hesitated because Alison Beech was right up beside him now and she was so beautiful and so confident and so magnetic that he didn't think anyone would even dare to try and kidnap her. 'He's trying to kidnap you,' Eddie said weakly. 'Really.'

Alison Beech stood by Scuttles' left shoulder. His mother was on his right. The Lord Mayor peered over his mother, shaking his head. 'This is ridiculous,' he was saying, 'absolutely ridiculous!'

His mum tried to say something on his behalf. But it wasn't very convincing. 'I'm sure he was just—'

'He was just about to break the fire alarm,' said Scuttles. 'Think of the panic that would have caused, all these poor sick patients . . .'

Eddie strained against Scuttles' hand, but he was held firmly in place. He looked at Alison Beech in desperation. 'Please. You have to believe me, they're trying to kidnap you.'

For a moment Eddie saw genuine fear in her eyes, but she covered it quickly. She pointed at herself. 'Little me?' she said, then raised her hands in mock panic for the benefit of the small audience gathered around her. 'Now, why would anyone want to do that?'

They all burst into laughter, everyone with the exception of Scuttles, Eddie and Eddie's mum.

'Oh, Eddie,' his mum whispered. 'How could you?'

'I'm telling the truth! You have to believe me! They're waiting on the fourth floor!'

Alison Beech smiled sweetly at him. 'Well they'll have a long wait – because I'm not even going to the fourth floor – am I, Mr Scuttles?'

'No ma'am,' said Scuttles.

'But—!' Eddie began.

His mother cut him off. 'Eddie, I think you've done enough damage,' she said, her face as sad as he'd ever seen it, and a very deep shade of red.

Alison Beech suddenly clapped her hands together. 'Oh, just let him go, no harm done!' Then she turned on her heel. 'Come now, chop, chop, no time to lose! I've all this money to give away, and I haven't seen half the place yet! Lead on, Sister, lead on!'

Mum, who wasn't a Sister at all, but an ordinary nurse, gave Eddie the frostiest of frosty looks, then smiled at Alison Beech, and led her and the rest of the party away, leaving Eddie pinned to the wall with Scuttles breathing fire over him.

Eddie had never seen his mother look so disappointed.

'Mum!' He called after her. 'I'm sorry! I didn't mean to ruin—'

Scuttles slapped his hand down over Eddie's mouth. 'Shut it, rat-boy!'

He kept his hand there until Alison Beech and the rest of the party had disappeared around a bend in the corridor, then removed it. Eddie tried to push away again, but Scuttles wouldn't let him move.

'You heard her,' Eddie said, 'you're to let me go.'

'Yeah, I heard. But I'm in charge of security here, and the only place you're going is my office, and you'll stay there until Alison Beech is off the premises. Kidnap indeed! You need medication, boy!'

He grabbed Eddie by the collar and began to lead him away.

Eddie walked with him for several metres, but he wasn't finished yet. Far from it.

He knew he was right.

Maybe he'd got some of the details wrong.

But *something* was going on, and Scuttles wanted to lock him up until it was all over.

Now there is a simple rule for making a fully-grown adult male let you go.

It never, ever fails. And all kids should know this. Most of them do.

You whack him in the willy.

So Eddie whacked him in the willy.

Scuttles screamed, let him go, and sank to his knees, groaning. Eddie took off.

But Scuttles wasn't long in following. Maybe he was wearing extra strong security guard underpants or something, but Eddie had barely made the stairs before Scuttles burst through the doors behind him.

'You stop now!' Scuttles screamed, and then screamed equally loudly into his radio for further assistance.

Eddie made the second floor landing, and Scuttles made a dive for him – missed!

Eddie made the first floor landing, and Scuttles grabbed for him again and just caught the back of his jacket, but Eddie pulled hard and Scuttles lost his grip on it, then slipped on one of the steps and went down hard on his bum.

Eddie sprinted away, but Scuttles was determined not to let him go.

An alarm began to sound, a loud wail that could wake the dead.

Well – almost wake the dead. Because when Eddie crashed through the doors of the mortuary the dead were still very dead on their tables, with Barney happily washing away.

Eddie tore across the room. 'Hiya, Barney,' he said and dived into the tunnel entrance.

A moment later Scuttles crashed through the doors, hesitated for a moment as he saw Barney raising a dead leg, then sprinted towards the still swinging tunnel doors.

'Hey!' Barney shouted. 'You can't just—'

'Yes I can!' Scuttles shouted back, and pulled himself through the doors after Eddie.

Nineteen

It was only a short slither to the fresh air beyond, but to Eddie it felt like a million miles. Scuttles huffed and puffed as he dragged his ample frame along the narrow tunnel behind him, shouting and cursing at him the whole way.

There is a saying about there being light at the end of the tunnel, which means that in bad times there is also usually a glimmer of hope, that you shouldn't give up. But to Eddie, even though he really *could* see light at the end of the tunnel, there was no hope at all.

Sure, he would get out of the tunnel ahead of Scuttles, and sure, he might avoid the other security guards, and passing members of the public, alerted by the alarm which continued to reverberate across the hospital, and yes he'd probably be able to scramble over a wall to the outside world, and yes, perhaps he'd avoid getting beaten up by the Reservoir Pups waiting outside. But the one thing that was absolutely certain was that eventually, even if he hid out on the streets for the rest of the day, the week or the month, eventually he would have to go home and confront his mother. She would disown him, as his father had done, she would turn him out of their home, or have him adopted, or fostered, or sent to a home for orphans or juvenile delinquents. He would plead his case – that he had been acting in her best interests, trying to protect her from an outrageous kidnap plot which somehow hadn't quite happened. Maybe his very presence had caused Scuttles to abandon his plan. Whatever the truth was, she wouldn't believe it. Maybe if he . . . oh, what was the use. He was done for. He was really done for.

Eddie reached the end of the tunnel and tumbled out on to the footpath. The alarm was sounding even louder. The white van was a lot closer than he remembered, but there was no sign of the driver. Eddie charged to his left, then pressed himself into a small alcove fifteen metres along, just as Scuttles emerged from the mouth of the tunnel. He was about to turn in Eddie's direction when he was stopped suddenly by a most unexpected sound.

A baby crying.

Scuttles looked behind him, he looked at the van almost directly in front of him, he looked to his left and his right. No baby.

And then it cried again.

Slowly Scuttles raised his eyes until he was looking directly *above* him.

A tiny baby, squeezed into a large black sock, was sliding at great speed down a cable which was stretched from a window on the fourth floor to the top of the white van. A pole was sticking out of the van's roof and, as the baby reached it, zooming in over Scuttles' head, two thick white hands reached up and removed it from the cable and carried it down inside the vehicle.

Eddie, squinting out of his hiding place, was absolutely stunned – although not as stunned as Scuttles clearly was. The security chief stood frozen, still looking up at the cable – and at the other six babies that were speeding down it and over his head.

Babies.

They're kidnapping babies.

I got it all wrong. They were using Alison Beech as a distraction. That's why they needed the security codes, to get into the maternity wing.

Scuttles finally shook himself, and made a grab for his radio.

But before he could say a word, the side doors of the minivan shot open, the driver jumped out and punched Scuttles once, very hard, on the top of his forehead. Scuttles' legs buckled under him. As he dropped, the driver caught him and bundled him into the back of the van. Then he pulled the door shut and a moment later his hands reappeared through the hole in the roof, just in time to retrieve the next baby.

Eddie followed the path of the cable up to the fourth floor. He could see Baldy framed in the window, attaching yet another baby. In a moment it began its journey through the air, crying its little heart out, even as the van driver held his hands out to receive the next one.

Altogether Eddie counted twelve babies before Baldy climbed on to the cable himself and slipped down it on to the roof of the van. A moment later Muscles raced down it too. Together they pushed the pole back down through the roof, then jumped down on to the pavement and clambered back into the van. Then it took off at speed, leaving the cable dangling from the window above, the alarm sounding in the background, and the screams of frightened mothers beginning to reverberate around the Royal Victoria Hospital.

Twenty

Eddie had a simple choice to make.

He could stay where he was, wait for the police to arrive, and tell them exactly what he had seen. He could identify the kidnappers and had instantly memorised the licence plate and make of the getaway vehicle. He would be a star witness. There might even be a reward.

Or he could give chase.

If he waited the kidnappers could just disappear. They could be holed up somewhere for weeks, demanding money for the babies' safe return. Some of the babies might even die. They might get sick or be injured if the police tried to storm wherever they were being held.

Really there was no choice at all.

He had to move quickly. The van had already disappeared around the corner. Eddie was a good runner, but he wasn't *that* good. But Barney's bike was sitting beside the entrance to the tunnel. Eddie raced up to it, praying that Barney was the only person in the whole city who didn't lock his bike.

But there was a chain. Eddie cursed. He grabbed at it in frustration – and it came away in his hands. He would have laughed if the situation hadn't been so serious – Barney had probably lost the key to his security chain, but still tied it around the bike in the vain hope that a thief wouldn't look too closely at it.

Eddie sped after the van.

As he rounded the corner he saw that it had already smashed through the security barrier. As Eddie pedalled madly after it, the stunned security guards tried to block his way, now wary of everyone and everything. But Eddie was good, and they were overweight. He swayed this way and that, just managing to avoid their flailing arms.

The van had circled the roundabout outside the hospital, thankfully not turning on to the motorway, where it would have been impossible to give chase, but turning instead into the Rivers. They were probably hoping to lose any pursuers in the tight winding streets of the housing estate. But this was no bad thing for Eddie as he gave chase – the streets were so narrow the van wouldn't be able to go all that fast, it gave him a slight chance of catching up.

But barely had his front wheel passed the

entrance to the estate before he saw Bacon and Bap hurling abuse – and several stones – at the passing van. Clearly Bacon hadn't forgiven the driver for kicking him. Eddie screamed to a halt beside them.

'What do you want, Curly,' Bacon spat, 'some of this?' and he brandished another stone at Eddie.

'I want . . .' Eddie said breathlessly, '. . . you to help me catch that van.'

'And why would we want to do that?' Bap snarled, coming up close to Eddie.

'Because they've kidnapped twelve babies.'

'They've what?'

'They've kidnapped twelve babies! I swear to God!'

Bacon looked at him incredulously. 'What're you talking about?'

'You know you're not allowed around here, Curly,' Bap warned. 'We should beat you to a pulp.'

'I know, I know . . . but listen . . . just listen.' There was no mistaking it – the air was alive with the sound of police sirens racing towards the hospital. 'I'm telling you, they've stolen babies from the hospital, we have to get after them.'

Bap looked at Bacon, Bacon looked at Bap, and they both nodded. 'We haven't any wheels,' Bacon said. 'You follow them, we'll send help.' And with that he raised a walkie-talkie to his mouth and began to talk.

Eddie took off again, forcing his tiring legs to go faster, to go longer. The white van was just disappearing in the distance. As he rode, taking corners at speed, mounting kerbs, forcing innocent pedestrians to dive out of his way, always keeping the van just within his field of vision, Eddie was gradually joined by other Reservoir Pups – some on bikes, some on scooters, some running as fast as leopards, one was even on a small motorbike. They twisted this way and that in their pursuit of the van. Word was spreading like wildfire. Up ahead he could see kids pouring out of houses, joining the chase. And then there were others, coming out of alleys, coming out of boarded-up wrecks of buildings before the van had even reached them. They stood in the middle of the street, blocking its path, only diving out of the way at the very final moment as it refused to brake. The kids picked themselves up and joined in the chase as Eddie swept up with the pack of mounted Reservoir Pups behind him. He became aware of a great yelping cry enveloping them, a cry like that of starving wolves in pursuit of a mighty bear, a bear that could tear them to pieces one by one, but surely couldn't withstand so many of them.

They were gaining on the van. The streets here were tighter, it just couldn't keep up the same speed without crashing. But the kids could. They knew every bump and every short cut. They raced along alleys, they leapt over walls, all the time getting closer and closer. It was the most dangerous thing Eddie had ever done, but he felt exhilarated, like he was leading an army into battle.

And then, just as he was growing confident that they really could stop the van, rescue the babies, the gang following behind him came to a sudden halt. Dozens and dozens of them, drawing up in a line behind him, refusing to go an inch further even as the van was almost within touching distance.

Eddie braked and shouted back at them: 'What are you doing? We have them!'

Sean, the crop-haired boy who'd taken charge of Eddie's bike at Reservoir Pups' HQ, shook his head sadly. 'We can't go any further.'

'What're you talking about?!' Eddie shouted. 'They're getting away!'

'This is the end of our territory. Down there belongs to the Andytown Albinos. We go in there, and we're dead meat.'

'But you have to! This is the crime of the century!'

'We can't.'

'There'll be a huge reward! There's bound to be! Come on!' Eddie vainly tried to wave them forward, but the crop-haired boy turned his bike and began to wheel it away back into the estate. And everyone else went with him.

Eddie stared after them, aghast.

'I don't believe you!' he screamed after them. 'You . . . you . . . chickens!'

Sean stopped his bike then and looked back. 'We're not chickens, we're following Captain Black's orders, and we're preserving the peace. If you cross into Andytown you're breaking the agreement and they'll beat you to within an inch of your life. And because you've called us chickens, if you try crossing the Rivers again – we'll take that final inch, understood?'

Sean again joined the retreat of the Reservoir Pups.

Eddie glared after them, then suddenly convulsed with anger, shouted: 'I don't care about any agreement! It has nothing to do with me! And you *are* bloody chickens!'

Then he took a deep breath, aimed his bike towards Andytown, and continued his pursuit of the baby-snatchers.

Twenty-One

Andytown wasn't as big as the Rivers, but it had just as big a reputation for casual violence. Central to that reputation was the gang known as the Albinos. Eddie had seen the look of fear in Sean's eyes, and heard the respect in Captain Black's voice when he had mentioned the gang. Now Eddie sped along the streets of Andytown, which were straighter, more modern than the dark curling sprawl of the Rivers. There, there could be a surprise around every corner; here, there weren't many corners – which was lucky, because in the far distance he could just about see the white van of the baby-snatchers. Gritting his teeth, fighting against the intense pains in his legs, Eddie raced on, deliberately ignoring everyone he passed on the way. To look anyone in the eye was to court trouble, to invite a challenge.

Andytown was cut in two by this one main thoroughfare. It was flat and Eddie's progress was only occasionally troubled by potholes, glass or the burned-out wreck of a stolen car. Nobody tried to stop him. A couple of kids shouted at him, but he kept eyes front and reached the far side of the estate in just a few minutes. He paused for a moment to catch a relieved breath, then stared down a slight incline towards a large industrial estate: factories, warehouses, car showrooms. He remembered this place from the map in Captain Black's office. He knew that although nobody lived here, it still fell within the territory controlled by the Andytown Albinos. But it wasn't half as frightening. He could see that paths had been worn between the different factories and warehouses, probably by kids like himself on bikes. From his elevated position he could tell that if he stuck to those paths he could quickly gain ground on the baby-snatchers' van which was now crawling along, stuck in heavy traffic on the single main road which served the industrial estate.

Eddie surged forward. Barney's bike was built for just this kind of rough terrain. It leapt over mounds of earth, it careered along makeshift bridges, it seemed to glide as Eddie steered it up steep inclines. For long stretches as Eddie raced along ditches and miniature valleys he lost sight of the van, and then smiled to himself each time as he reached higher ground and saw how much closer he was getting to it.

Finally Eddie pulled the bike up a grass bank and on to the main road. He was less than a hundred metres from the baby-snatchers' van. Now, if he could just reach the lorry that was sitting in front of it, and somehow persuade the driver to block the van's escape route, then surely . . .

But suddenly the van pulled off to the right and entered a narrow slip road. Eddie followed, passing a large sign which said: 'STRICTLY PRIVATE' in large red letters. This didn't deter him for one moment, but it did cause him to slow down. This was a different kind of road, curved so he couldn't quite see what was ahead. He approached each bend cautiously, his heart drumming, until finally the road straightened and he saw a massive warehouse ahead of him, completely surrounded by a high wire fence. There appeared to be only one entrance, a set of double gates through which the van had already passed and which were now being closed by Muscles. Eddie quickly ducked back beyond the bend so that he wouldn't be spotted, and only ventured out again when he heard the van door slam. He watched as the vehicle approached the front of the warehouse; a door was slid open from within and the van disappeared inside. A moment later the door was shut again.

So – they think they're safe. But actually, they're trapped, he thought excitedly.

All he had to do now was to alert the police – but what if he left to find a phone box or stop a passing car, and the baby-snatchers disappeared again while he was gone? Perhaps they were just in the warehouse to change vehicles. Or nappies. Perhaps there was another exit, perhaps they had driven straight through the warehouse, and would emerge in a few minutes on the other side in a different van?

Half of him was saying *Go now, get help*.

The other half was saying *Stay, make sure they don't escape*.

But, as ever in his short life, when called upon to make an important decision, that decision was taken out of his hands. From behind him, a voice said, 'Are you lost, or just stupid?'

Eddie turned to find a girl of about his own age standing there, her hands bunched into fists. She was wearing a black zip-up jacket, black jeans and a black baseball cap. And the black was all the more startling because it was in total contrast to her skin which was deathly pale. Whiter than white. Her hair, tied up and sprouting in a ponytail from the back of her cap was also white – not blonde, but white. But it was her eyes that really spooked him. They weren't blue or black or green or brown like every person he had ever met. They were just visible under the shadow of the peak of her cap, and they were pink. Pink. She looked like something that should have been lying on one of Barney's tables, ready for a good wash and then burial, but she was undoubtedly alive, because she stepped right up to him.

'Well?' she demanded. 'What're you playing at?'

'I—' Eddie falteringly began, but she cut him off.

'Don't you know where you are?'

'I—'

'Have you never heard of the Andytown Albinos?'

'Yes, but—'

'Don't you know what we do to anyone we find on our land?'

'Yes, I—'

'We tear them limb from limb. And then we post those limbs back to their homes so everyone'll know we're not to be messed with.'

'I'm not—'

'See this phone?' She held up a mobile phone. 'I

push one button on this, there'll be fifty of us here in twenty seconds. So don't even think about trying to escape.'

'I wasn't,' Eddie said.

'Then what do you want?'

Eddie swallowed. 'I want to borrow your phone.'

This surprised her. 'What?' she said.

'Can I borrow your phone? Please. It's important.'

Her pale eyes narrowed suspiciously. 'What's so important?'

'I have to phone the police.'

The girl laughed suddenly. 'You think they're going to help you? They're scared of *us*, not the other way round.'

'No – really, it's not for that, it's . . .' He took a deep breath and glanced back towards the warehouse. 'That's where they are. The baby-snatchers.'

'The who?'

'It's a gang, they've stolen about a dozen babies from the hospital, they're in there, in that warehouse. If we call the police now we can catch them.'

'If *we* call the police? I don't think so.'

'Please.'

'You expect me to believe that rubbish?'

'It's true, I swear to God.'

'You can swear to whoever you want, I still don't believe you.'

'Really it is – I . . . look, I've heard all about you, the Andytown . . .' and he couldn't quite bring himself to say Albinos, looking as he was directly at the most fearsome albino girl he'd ever met in his life – indeed the *only* albino girl he'd met in his life – so he said, 'the Andytown gang, I know how dangerous you are, you think I'd risk coming in here if it wasn't absolutely vital? I'm trying to save those babies. Please. Help me.'

She looked at him. He looked away. He couldn't meet those eyes.

'How much?' she asked.

'How much what?'

'How much will you pay to use my phone?'

'It's an emergency!'

'So what? You still haven't a phone. So how much?'

'I haven't any money.'

'Yeah, sure.'

'I haven't, I really haven't, now please let me use your phone.'

'The bike then.'

'The bike then what?'

'Give me your bike.'

'For a phone call!'

'Well, if it's that important, it shouldn't be a problem.'

Eddie glared at her. She wasn't only spooky, she was as tough as nails. He had no choice. And in a moment he had no bike. He handed it over to her. She gave him the phone.

'One call,' she snapped.

Eddie nodded. He dialled 999 and asked for the police. A gruff, harassed-sounding voice said: 'Yes?' and Eddie quickly told him he knew where the stolen babies were.

The policeman listened, then said: 'Are you winding me up?'

'No! I swear to God!'

'How old are you?'

'What difference does it make! I know where they are!'

'Yes, son, and you're about the hundredth person to call us claiming to know where they are. Do you know why? I'll tell you why. Because this gang was driving a white van, and do you know how many white vans there are in this city? Thousands!'

'But it's *this* white van,' Eddie remonstrated. 'I followed them, they haven't been out of my sight. I know exactly where they are. Please. You have to come.'

The policeman sighed at the other end of the line. 'Frankly, I think you're lying through your teeth. But it's my sworn duty to follow up every call. So we'll send a car out to check, but it won't be for a while, we've a lot of other calls to deal with. Just stay where you are, we'll get there as soon as we can.'

The policeman cut the line. Eddie stared at the phone. 'They don't believe me,' he said.

The albino girl stepped forward and snapped the phone out of his hand. 'Surprise, surprise,' she said.

'But they're coming anyway.'

The girl shrugged, and picked up the bike. 'Well, I'm not hanging around for them,' she said. 'And you should scram as well, if you know what's good for you.'

She climbed on and rode off, without looking back.

Eddie sighed. He had lost two bikes in one day. And one of them wasn't even his.

But he had survived his first encounter with the

Andytown Albinos, and the police were on the way to rescue the stolen babies.

His life was definitely taking a turn for the better.

Twenty-Two

Eddie walked back to the top of the road and sat on the kerb just behind the large STRICTLY PRIVATE sign. No other vehicles arrived at or left the warehouse. He saw nothing further of the Andytown Albino. After forty-five minutes a police vehicle finally arrived, a dull grey armour-plated Land-Rover with wire mesh across the front windscreen to stop people throwing stones through it. A burly police officer wound down the driver's window and introduced himself as Constable O'Rourke. He told Eddie to climb in the back. As Eddie went behind the Land-Rover the rear door opened and another officer, who said he was Constable Doyle, gave Eddie a hand up.

'Well,' said Constable Doyle, 'let's get to the bottom of this.'

They drove down the lane and stopped before the set of locked metal gates. There was an intercom system in place, and Constable O'Rourke spoke into it. A moment later Baldy appeared from within the warehouse, walking a massive Rottweiler on what looked like an inadequate chain. He spoke to the constable through the gates. Eddie couldn't quite hear what was being said, but from where he was sitting behind the driver's seat, he could see Baldy smiling and nodding with Constable O'Rourke. A moment later O'Rourke climbed back into the vehicle while Baldy opened the gates and then followed the Land-Rover across the tarmac to the warehouse's huge sliding door.

Constable Doyle climbed out of the rear doors, then signalled for Eddie to follow. He hesitated. 'It'll be fine,' Doyle said, and gave him a wink. Eddie reluctantly climbed down and stood between the two cops. The Rottweiler growled at him. Baldy, without giving Eddie a second glance, then led the three of them through a side door into the warehouse, where they were quickly joined by Muscles. The dog growled at Eddie again. Baldy explained to Muscles what the police wanted. 'They don't have a warrant or nothing,' he said, 'but I don't see what harm it can do.'

'Nah – feel free to wander around,' said Muscles. 'Twelve babies, you say? I got one at home, and that's more than enough for me – bloody nightmare he is.'

Muscles laughed. Baldy laughed. The two police officers laughed. Eddie turned and faced the warehouse.

It seemed to him to be as large as a football stadium. Vast, dark and dusty. The inside was split into rows of shelves, and each row stretched as far as the eye could see, and rose so high that the tops of them were lost in the gloom. Each shelf was stacked with large cardboard boxes, thousands of them, so many that Eddie couldn't even hazard a guess as to how many. It was like a warehouse that supplied other warehouses. There was no way that two police officers could search a place this big, not unless they stayed for a week.

'You're going to need more people,' Eddie said quietly.

Constable O'Rourke glanced down at him. 'We'll be fine.'

'So what is it you do here, exactly?' Constable Doyle asked.

Muscles shrugged. 'Pile stuff up, then ship it out. Twenty-four hours a day, three hundred and sixty-five days a year.'

Doyle strolled across to the closest shelf and peered inside a box. He lifted out a bottle of shampoo.

'If your missus fancies a free bottle,' Baldy said, 'we won't say nothing.'

Doyle smiled, but replaced the bottle in the box. He turned back to O'Rourke. 'Okay, let's take a look.'

O'Rourke moved forward to join his partner, and Muscles went with him, leaving Eddie standing alone with Baldy for a moment. Eddie stared straight ahead, aware that Baldy was looking at him, then jumped as Baldy's hand came down suddenly on his shoulder. The dog wasn't growling this time. It was snarling.

'You know what happens to troublemakers?' Baldy hissed. Eddie didn't wait to find out. He shrugged Baldy's hand off and darted forward, quickly catching up with the two police constables and their guide. When he glanced back Baldy had disappeared. He must have looked frightened because Doyle glanced down at him and said, 'Okay, son?'

Eddie nodded and kept as close to the police officers as he could while Muscles gave them a tour of the warehouse. He led them down aisle after aisle; turning left, turning right at junctions, there was even a small roundabout in the middle of the warehouse which Muscles said helped with the traffic on days when they were particularly busy. This wasn't one of those days. Muscles said it was the company's annual holiday, so there was only a skeleton staff.

Every once in a while Constable O'Rourke made them stop and stand quietly for a few moments. Muscles looked at him like he was mad, but Eddie knew what he was doing – he was listening for the sound of babies crying.

But there was nothing, so they walked on. Five, ten, fifteen, twenty minutes, and Eddie could tell that the cops were tiring of their fruitless search.

Muscles kept up a constant babble about kids and work and sport, all the while leading them this way and that through this huge cardboard city – a city in which no babies appeared to be living.

And then, just as they turned into a different aisle, Eddie spotted something. It was the merest flash of white, only visible because something had bumped into one of the boxes and knocked it out of alignment with the others. Eddie pressed his face to the gap, and saw the back of a white van.

His heart was thundering now. They were going to catch them.

'Over here!' Eddie shouted. The two cops and Muscles now moved quickly back towards him.

Eddie pointed to the gap and O'Rourke bent down to it. He nodded slightly, then glanced at Doyle. 'White van, right enough,' he said.

Doyle took a look for himself, then they turned together and faced Muscles.

'So what's it doing hidden in there?' Doyle asked.

Muscles shrugged. He didn't look at all worried, although Eddie was sure that inside he was panicked. He was about to be arrested!

'Well?' O'Rourke asked.

'Dunno,' said Muscles. 'Nothing to do with me. Ask the boss.'

'Where is he?' asked Doyle.

'Right here.'

Eddie jumped. Baldy had somehow crept up on them.

'What seems to be the problem?' he asked. His voice was smooth and confident and Eddie realised that simply having two police officers with him was no guarantee of protection. The gang was bound to have weapons. They could easily overwhelm the cops and make their getaway. Doyle must have been thinking the same thing, because he suddenly drew his gun and said: 'White van, just what we're looking for. Let's have a nosey, eh?'

It was the only part of the United Kingdom where cops were allowed to carry guns – and Eddie was more than glad of it as he watched Baldy raise his hands in a peaceful gesture. 'Whatever you say, Constable, we don't want no trouble. If you'll just help me move these boxes.'

They moved several boxes, then bent down low to scramble through a small gap into a rectangular area which might have been formed naturally by the intersection of several rows of shelving – or been deliberately constructed as a space in which to hide things, things like a large white van with *Braxton Hicks Contractors* written on the side. It was the same van. It had to be. They stood looking at it for several moments, straining to hear the sound of tiny babies crying. But there was nothing. What if they were too late? What if they were all dead?

'You mean this old thing?' Baldy said. 'Sure it's just a decrepit old heap we use to store paint in.'

'Well, let's just take a look, shall we?' said Doyle. He nodded at O'Rourke, who drew his gun to cover Muscles and Baldy, then holstered his own gun and stepped up to the side doors of the vehicle. He reached up to the handle.

'Constable,' Baldy said, 'I wouldn't do that if I was you.'

Doyle didn't blink. 'I'm sure you wouldn't,' he replied, then pulled the door open.

He was immediately consumed by an avalanche of paint tins, most of them already open and half full. Although not for long.

Doyle let out a cry of surprise, then pain, then horror, as the dozens of tins and litres of paint swept over him, knocking him to the floor.

Everyone, including Eddie, stepped back to avoid the deluge.

After several long moments, when the cans which were rolling away had come to a halt, Constable Doyle slowly raised himself off the ground. He was covered from head to toe. He looked like a human rainbow. His police cap was white, his trousers were blue and pink and green, his tunic was yellow and brown and black and his face was white – though not as white as the face of the girl Eddie had met outside.

Constable Doyle was not a happy man.

'Like your new coat,' Muscles said, and both he and Baldy burst into laughter.

This did not make Doyle any happier.

'You shut your cake hole!' he bellowed.

But he was ignored. And O'Rourke was now finding it impossible not to laugh as well.

'Well, don't just stand there!' Doyle roared. 'Help me!'

O'Rourke holstered his gun and hurried across to give Doyle a hand.

Eddie took another step backwards.

Then another.

Doyle's white face and burning eyes snapped towards him. 'You! This is all your fault! I'll bloody have you! Wasting police time! Look at the state of me! I'll throw the bloody key away when I get my hands . . .'

But Eddie was already off and running.

Twenty-Three

When Eddie got home, he found his mum crying in the kitchen, a damp tissue balled up in one hand, the TV remote control in the other. She was flicking from channel to channel, watching the blanket coverage of the theft of twelve babies from the Royal Victoria Hospital.

The hysterical parents of the stolen babies were interviewed at length.

The managing director of the hospital was interviewed, doctors, nurses, porters and patients were asked to give their accounts of what had happened.

'They wanted to interview me,' Mum said, 'but I was too upset.'

Eddie put an arm around her and gave her a squeeze.

'I'm sure it'll all work out,' he said.

'You smell of paint,' Mum replied, but before he could come up with an explanation she let out a wail of despair as a photo of Bernard J. Scuttles, Head of Security, appeared in the corner of the screen. In the foreground, a grave-looking policeman called Chief Inspector Craig was making a statement to a crowded press conference.

'This is clearly a serious, evil crime perpetrated against the most defenceless of all God's creatures, our babies. Our hearts go out to the parents and relatives involved, and we have reassured them that we are leaving no stone unturned in our efforts to recover their little ones. We are currently following up a number of leads, and we would ask the public to be on the lookout for anything or anyone suspicious. However we would stress that these men may be armed and are certainly dangerous and should under no circumstances be approached. At this moment in time we would like to talk to one person in particular – Bernard J. Scuttles, Head of Security at the hospital here, who has not been seen since the babies were taken.'

A journalist shouted out: 'Is he your chief suspect?'

Chief Inspector Craig gave him a serious look and said: 'At this point in time we would just like to talk to him. Again, I should reiterate that these people should not be approached. They are highly dangerous.'

Mum let out another wail. 'They think Bernie's involved!'

Eddie wasn't sure what to think. He had been convinced that Scuttles was in on the plan to kidnap Alison Beech, although that hadn't been the plan at all. But the way Scuttles had chased him through the hospital, and then been pulled into the getaway van – well, that didn't look planned. That looked like Scuttles had been kidnapped. Or perhaps that was how it was meant to look. Perhaps the security cameras in the area would show what appeared to be Scuttles being kidnapped – but was actually all a set-up to get him off the hook.

The Lord Mayor of Belfast appeared on screen, condemning the baby-snatchers.

The Prime Minister appeared from 10 Downing Street, promising that the babies would be recovered.

The Queen released a statement from Buckingham Palace offering her support for the grieving parents.

An expert on kidnapping said that while it wasn't unusual for a single baby to be kidnapped, it was highly unusual for twelve babies to be taken at the same time. He also said that babies were usually taken from rich families so that a ransom could be demanded, but that none of the parents involved were thought to be wealthy – nor had any money been asked for. He was most perplexed.

For the next couple of hours Eddie and his mum sat at the kitchen table watching the portable. It grew dark outside. Every once in a while his mum would say, 'It's terrible,' or 'It's dreadful,' or 'Those poor little kids.' At around eight o'clock there was a sudden flurry of activity on screen as reporters scrambled to cover a surprise press conference by Alison Beech.

She wiped away a tear as she stepped up to the microphone.

Mum wiped away a tear as well.

'This has been a dreadful day for all of us,' Alison Beech started. 'A day which began so full of hope in this very hospital. The pleasure I experienced in donating so much money to this tragically under-funded establishment was swept away in an instant by this outrageous – horrific – crime. Those poor, innocent little children. What is this world coming to?' She shook her head sadly. Then looked suddenly harder as she stared into the camera. 'I am tonight announcing a reward of one million pounds for anyone who can provide information that will lead to the safe return of these babies.

Please, if you know anything, get in touch with the police – or, if you feel that you can't talk to them, then talk to me, there is a special number you can call, which is appearing at the bottom of your screens right now, and my people will be manning the phones twenty-four hours a day until these little babies are returned to us. Thank you.'

She smiled bravely, then the cameras followed her as she moved away from the microphone. She was quickly joined by her entourage and escorted towards a fleet of waiting limousines.

Mum was writing the number on the screen down on the back of a cereal box. 'You never know,' she said.

Eddie went to bed just before midnight, leaving his mum in exactly the same position in the kitchen, glued to the screen.

Naturally, he couldn't sleep.

He lay on his back and stared at the ceiling, trying to work out why his life was so messed up, and how, when he tried to do good things, they always turned out bad. In a matter of days he had changed from being a nice young fella from the country into a burglar, a liar and a bully. He had lost his father and made his mother miserable. He had made enemies of the Reservoir Pups and the Andytown Albinos, the security guards at the hospital and the police. He had been branded a coward by Captain Black. He had made one new friend in Barney, then stolen his bike. And had then given it away for the price of a phone call, a call which had landed him in even deeper water.

He found it difficult to think of anything positive that had come out of his move to the city.

And then it came to him.

He, of all the people in this dark, dangerous city, had the chance to receive one million pounds.

Because he had seen the baby-snatchers.

He knew what they looked like.

And, more importantly, he knew where they were.

Or thought he did.

Muscles and Baldy – and quite possibly Scuttles – had stolen the babies. He had followed them to the warehouse, but the police had been unable to find the babies. It didn't mean they weren't there. It was a massive place, there could be hundreds of hiding places.

They *had* to be there.

But what to do?

He thought of the number on the back of the

Frosties box Mum had jotted down off the TV – why not phone Alison Beech's people and tell them?

But they would only inform the police, and they would say they'd already searched the warehouse, and by the way was it a really annoying troublemaking kid who called you?

No – he wouldn't phone Alison Beech.

Instead he sat up and put his trainers back on.

The fact was that all along Eddie knew what he really had to do. It just took a while for him to accept it, because thus far everything he had put his hand to had ended in disaster. And this plan had the potential to be an even bigger catastrophe than all of his previous efforts. But there was no alternative.

He had to go back to the warehouse.

And he had to go now.

Twenty-Four

There was a fine rain falling as Eddie, wearing black jeans, a black T-shirt and a zip-up black jacket, jogged along the hard shoulder of the motorway which looped around the outside of the Rivers and then back along the edge of the industrial estate beyond Andytown. It was now the early hours of the morning, and there was very little traffic, so that when a car did come along, either towards him or from behind, he had plenty of warning of it and was able to duck down into the long grass which grew on the steep banks on either side of the carriageway.

It was probably around 2.30 am when Eddie finally came to a stop at the top of the narrow road leading down to the warehouse. He knelt down in the shelter of the STRICTLY PRIVATE sign and checked the contents of the schoolbag he had been carrying: a flashlight, his mum's video camera for collecting evidence, and her mobile phone for summoning assistance, a pair of pliers he hoped would double as wire cutters, half a pound of pork sausages, a penknife and a smoke bomb.

Of course, it wasn't really a smoke bomb. It was a small pink tablet which he had rescued from his father's garden shed before they'd moved to the city; when lit it emitted a blanket of smoke which was supposed to kill greenfly. Eddie, however, had always been aware of its wider uses and he and his mates had had great fun setting off smoke bombs in the woods around Groomsport.

That all seemed a very long while ago now.

Eddie hurried along the narrow road. As he had expected, the gates to the warehouse were heavily padlocked. Luckily the area was not well-lit, so he was able to slip unnoticed along the perimeter fence looking for the best place to cut the wire. But he didn't need to. About a hundred metres along he found a gap just large enough for him to squeeze through. Once inside he crouched down, peering into the darkness towards the massive outline of the warehouse, then darted forward.

He was about ten metres from the warehouse wall when he heard the low growl.

He froze.

The growl came again. From just in front of him.

He had no idea if dogs could see in the dark.

But they could certainly smell.

They could smell fear.

Sweat dripped down Eddie's back.

Cautiously he swung his schoolbag round and felt inside for the sausages. He pulled them out, then reached back in for his penknife.

In a moment he would either be feeding the massive Rottweiler, or fighting it.

It growled again – but this time it sounded slightly different, more inquisitive than threatening, before finally tailing off into a whine.

Eddie whispered into the darkness. 'Here we are – nice sausages . . . here we are . . .'

But the whine had become something else again . . . well, it sounded like snoring.

Eddie moved slowly forwards, the sausages held out in front of him as his first line of defence, the penknife shakily held only slightly behind them ready for the worst.

Then, in the darkness, he stepped on one of the dog's paws. Eddie leapt back, expecting a ferocious reaction, but the Rottweiler hardly made any response at all. He could now plainly see the outline of the dog lying flat out on the ground. He knelt beside it. It was fast asleep – but it didn't seem like a normal sleep. He even risked poking it, but still there was no reaction. Perhaps it was sick. Perhaps the baby-snatchers had drugged their own guard dog to stop its barking waking the babies. Whatever the cause, it was bad news for the dog, but good news for him.

Eddie stepped around the Rottweiler and hurried across to the warehouse wall. He flattened himself against it and listened again. There was the hum of a generator coming from somewhere but that was it. No other sounds from such a massive warehouse, a place Baldy had said was busy twenty-four hours a day. Clearly they'd shut it down to protect the babies.

He began to move along the wall, searching for some means of entry. There were a number of doors, but he hardly dared try them in case they were alarmed. There were windows as well, but again there was no way of telling if they were also hooked up to some massive alarm system. And then he caught a whiff of cardboard and perfume and realised that the window he was passing was open – no, not open, but *missing*. Even in the darkness it looked as if the glass had been cut out of the centre of the frame by an expert burglar.

It had probably been like that for a long time, gone unnoticed amidst the hectic activity of the warehouse. But it provided the perfect opportunity to breach the security of the warehouse. Eddie pulled himself up on to the window ledge, then carefully stepped through the window frame and lowered himself into the warehouse.

He had barely put his foot on the floor when something sharp was placed against his throat and a voice hissed: 'What the hell are *you* doing here?'

For a moment, Eddie thought he'd been caught by some kind of monster. There was only the barest minimum of light in the warehouse, so that when he turned very slowly, being careful not to let whatever was sticking into his neck cut into him, all he could see were two huge black goggle eyes, like those of a fly, magnified a thousand times.

'I said, what are you doing here?'

But there was something familiar about the voice. And straining in the poor light he could now see that on either side of the bug eyes the creature had extremely white hair.

'I—' Eddie began to say, but before he could get it out the creature let out a sigh and pushed its goggle eyes up on to the top of its head, leaving beneath them the perfectly normal, but extremely agitated face of his favourite Andytown Albino.

'You—' Eddie began again.

But again she cut him off. '*You*,' she said, 'are getting to be really annoying.'

And then somewhere in the distance there was the sound of an engine starting up and the Albino quickly dropped the shard of glass – for that's what it was – from Eddie's throat, pulled down the goggles again, and snapped, 'This way.'

She took his arm and began to lead him at speed along one of the aisles between the towering shelves of boxes. It was almost pitch black here, but she was leading him into the darkness without pause, whereas he was running with his arms stretched out in front of him, scared of banging into something. After a few minutes she stopped abruptly, listened, then pulled him through a narrow gap between two boxes. On the other side there was a large wooden crate which was padlocked. The girl quickly produced a key, slotted it into the lock, then pulled the side of the crate open. She ushered Eddie inside and pulled it closed behind them. For a moment they were in complete darkness, then a switch was flicked and the inside of the crate was suddenly illuminated.

There was a desk, chairs, a small fridge, a laptop, a television.

Eddie blinked in disbelief.

'Cool, yeah?' the Albino said. She opened the fridge. She produced a can of Coke and snapped it open. She took a long drink, then smiled, satisfied, at Eddie.

'I don't . . . understand . . .' Eddie spluttered. 'What . . . is this . . . Why are you here . . . What's that on your head . . . ?'

The Albino removed the goggles from her head and looked at them. 'Night vision glasses,' she said. She tossed them across to him. 'Haven't you ever tried night vision glasses? They're class.'

Eddie tried them on.

'They won't work in here, dummy, it's bright.'

'Oh,' Eddie said. He pushed them on to the top of his head. 'And what's this . . . ?' He nodded around the inside of the crate.

'This,' the Albino said proudly, 'is a forward command post of the Andytown Albinos.'

It was certainly impressive. 'Don't they ever . . . ?'

'Find us? No. And nor will they, unless stupid mutts like you get them curious. Every box in this warehouse has a code stuck on its side, and a box is only collected for distribution if that code comes up on a computer.' She stroked the top of the laptop. 'And we make sure it never will.'

'And all this stuff, it's stolen from the boxes, isn't it?'

'It's not stolen,' the Albino snapped. 'It's liberated. We can get anything we want, because it all comes through here at one time or another. This is our patch.'

'You drugged that dog, didn't you? And you cut out the glass from the window.' The Albino shrugged. 'But you can't be doing that every time you want to enter your – what is it – forward command post, surely?'

'Of course not, stupid.' She fixed him with a steady gaze. Then she seemed to come to some decision, nodding to herself. 'Used to be nobody ever bothered us here, but these last few weeks suddenly they stepped up the security, got dogs, installed alarms, so we guessed something was up. We just didn't know what. And now we do.'

'So you *do* believe me about the babies.'

The Albino shrugged. 'We believe Alison Beech is offering one million quid for their return. That's what interests us. And if you think you're getting any of it, you've another thing coming.'

Eddie shrugged. 'I just want to find the babies.'

'Well then,' the Albino said, 'you can tag along if

you want.' She bent to the desk in the middle of the crate and pulled open a drawer. She produced another set of night sight goggles, and two small hand-held devices. She tossed one at Eddie. He caught it, examined it, but had no idea what it was. Black, square and electronic. The back of it was stamped with 'Government Property – Do Not Remove'.

'What . . . ?' Eddie began.

'Thermal imaging,' said the Albino. 'Babies produce heat, and these little babies' – she held up her own device – 'detect it. If they're here, we'll find them.'

Twenty-Five

They climbed up into the dusty eaves of the warehouse. At first Eddie found it quite enjoyable, jumping from box to box, especially once he grew accustomed to the weird sensations that came with wearing the night vision glasses. They allowed him to see everything but imbued it all with a kind of green haze, like he was exploring a different planet. But the higher they went into the eaves, the more dangerous it became. In many places water had leaked through holes in the roof and rusted away at the shelves. Some had collapsed completely, causing boxes to sink into the shelves below, or the damp air had rotted away the cardboard and their contents had spilled on to those stacked beneath. The bitter smell of rancid perfume clung to everything.

The Albino beckoned for him to join her at the topmost point of one of the stacks of boxes and he pulled himself shakily up towards her. He could feel the whole rickety tower trembling beneath him. But it didn't seem to worry the Albino. 'Okay,' she whispered as he hunched down perilously beside her, 'you take that side, I'll take this.'

She had already shown him how to use the thermal imager. It was just a matter of switching on and scanning it slowly over a given area while watching a small rectangular screen. It was now showing the basic outlines of the shelves and the aisles as black lines – anything that was giving off heat would glow orange. Once detected it would be a simple case of following the black lines to the source of the heat.

He found something almost immediately – three glowing figures somewhere near the front of the building. He nudged the Albino – which wasn't a great idea, as she almost fell off the shelf.

'Watch it, for God's sake!' she hissed.

'Sorry, but look . . .'

She glanced at the screen and shook her head. 'The night shift, security guards. We're looking for twelve babies.'

Eddie nodded, and continued to scan. Then beside him the Albino gave a low exclamation. He peered over her shoulder and she pointed at a group of small orange spots glowing out of their dark surroundings.

'Is that them?'

'Shhhhh.' She was counting. 'Fifteen.' Her brow furrowed. 'Too many.'

'Could be twelve babies, plus their guards.'

'Or it could be a nest of rats.' She quickly scanned the rest of her section, then shook her head. 'We have to be sure.' She looked at Eddie – two goggle-eyed monsters checking each other out. 'Are you sure you're up for this?' she asked. 'It could get dangerous. And with you not being in a gang, I've no way of knowing whether you'll turn chicken on me or not.'

'Don't you worry about me.'

She raised a doubtful eyebrow, then led the climb back down to ground level, moving with an agility and confidence that left Eddie lagging far behind. She was obviously on familiar ground; when he did reach the floor he found her tapping her foot impatiently. She turned quickly then and began running along the dark aisles. Eddie was soon matching her stride for stride, turning left or right according to the directions on her thermal imager.

Then they heard it.

A baby's cry.

The Albino examined the imager, nodded to herself, then signalled for Eddie to follow. She led him into the next aisle. Slowly they inched along until they were sure the babies were just on the other side of the wall of boxes. But they were so tightly packed that there were no gaps they could see through. The girl pointed up. They would have to climb again. Eddie nodded. She led him further along the aisle until they came upon a less uniform series of boxes. The Albino raised her leg expectantly. Eddie hesitated for a moment, then folded his hands together to give her a leg-up. When she had pulled herself on to the first shelf, she turned and reached down to heave him up to join her. At least they were now working as a team.

They climbed as far up as they could, then began to make their way along the very top tier. The shelving was just as rusted and creaky as before and they had to proceed with renewed caution – not only out of fear of discovery, but in case they caused a shelf to collapse and debris to fall on the helpless babies below.

Finally they pulled themselves up on to the top row of boxes, pushed up their night vision glasses, and peered down –

– at twelve babies in twelve cots and Bernard J. Scuttles wearing only his underpants and a leather strap around his ankle connected to a chain that secured him to a metal spike which was sunk in the concrete floor. The chain was just long enough to allow him to reach the cots and what looked like a table normally used for wallpapering, but which now supported dozens of little plastic bottles and a large container of what Eddie presumed was formula milk. At the other end of the room – it was actually a rectangle formed by shelves of boxes – Muscles and Baldy sat at a smaller table, drinking coffee and playing cards. They looked up from time to time as Scuttles shuffled forward, filled a bottle then carefully lifted a gurgling baby from its cot and began to feed it. It looked as if the feeding was never ending, and even from their lofty position they could see that Scuttles was shattered.

When another of the babies began to cry, Muscles didn't even look up from his cards, but merely snapped: 'Sort that out, Bernard.'

'I'm already doing this one,' said Scuttles, his voice both weak and desperate. 'You could give me a hand.'

Muscles and Baldy looked at each other, and then gave Scuttles a round of applause. They burst into laughter.

'Just do it,' Baldy ordered, 'or we'll bust your legs.'

Scuttles gently removed the bottle from the baby

in his arms, but it wasn't ready to give it up and immediately started to wail, which caused the other baby to cry louder. Then, one by one, the others joined in. Even listening to it from the roof of the warehouse it was unbelievably loud and annoying.

Baldy and Muscles had a simple solution. They plugged in earphones and switched on Walkmans leaving Scuttles to flail about trying to quieten the babies' screams by himself.

Eddie carefully opened his bag and removed his mum's video camera.

As he raised it the Albino hissed: 'What are you doing?'

'Evidence,' Eddie whispered. 'The police will never believe us, but if we can show them then they'll—'

'We're not calling the police.'

'What? We have to, the babies—'

'We're calling Alison Beech, she's the one offering the reward. Give me that.' She pulled the video camera out of his hands. 'You forget where you are, Sonny Boy, this is Andytown Albino territory, we control the evidence, we get the reward. If you're lucky we'll slip you a couple of hundred quid for your trouble. Now, how do you work this?'

But Eddie's eyes were fixed on the room below.

'You don't need to phone Alison Beech,' he said.

The Albino, holding the camera at an angle to catch what little light there was so she could examine the controls, replied with a testy: 'Don't tell me what to do you little . . .'

But she trailed off as she saw the look of horror on Eddie's face. She followed his gaze down the stacked shelves, across the concrete floor, past the twelve wailing babies, the overwhelmed Scuttles and the two heavies tapping their feet in time to the music to where a narrow gap had now opened between the boxes, a gap which was filled by Alison Beech.

She stepped into the room, her figure tightly hugged by a black dress. She stood confidently on eight-inch stiletto heels and smiled magnificently at the twin rows of cots.

'My little babies,' she squealed.

Twenty-Six

The Albino was so shocked by Alison Beech's appearance that her hand involuntarily reached out towards Eddie, looking for support and reassurance in the darkness high above the stolen babies. But then she remembered who she was and what she was about and withdrew it before there was any contact, before in fact Eddie could grasp it, because he was reaching out as well, feeling exactly the same things. They blinked at each other awkwardly for several moments, then Eddie whispered quickly: 'What is she doing here?'

'Shhhh,' said the Albino.

'But why would she—'

'Shhh,' said the Albino again, and this time she did reach out to him, and nipped him on the leg. Eddie stifled a cry of pain. 'Just *listen*,' she said.

Down below, Muscles and Baldy were now hovering behind Alison Beech as she moved along each row of cots, peering in at and poking each baby in turn.

'Oh, they're so cute,' she cooed. 'Oh, they're so

lovely, so soft.' She lifted one out of its cot and kissed the top of its head. Then her nose crinkled up. 'What's that smell?' she snapped.

'Poo,' said Muscles.

Alison Beech immediately held the baby out to him. 'Well, do something about it.'

Muscles took the baby, then turned with it towards Scuttles. 'Hey, Bernie!' he shouted, then hurled the baby up into the air.

It was too shocked to scream.

But the Albino wasn't. She was just about to let go with a horrified yell when Eddie clamped his hand down over her mouth.

She struggled against him for just a moment.

Neither of them were able to take their eyes off the baby as Scuttles dived across the floor of the warehouse and caught it just before it hit the ground at the very limit of the chain that tethered him to the spike.

Scuttles sank to his knees and hugged the baby to his chest. Muscles and Baldy were laughing their heads off.

Alison Beech wasn't exactly amused, but neither was she particularly angry. 'Please try and be careful with them, little piggies don't grow on trees.'

They immediately stopped laughing. 'Yes, ma'am,' they said obediently, 'sorry ma'am.'

It was too much for Scuttles. Clutching the baby to his chest he shouted, 'You have all the money in the world! Why would you need to steal these little babies?'

Alison Beech wasn't used to being addressed in such a manner. Her brow furrowed and her eyes narrowed and she came right up close to him, until her scarlet lips were a millimetre from his and her perfume enveloped him like a poisonous fog. 'Because I can,' she purred. And then she laughed, and at that moment Eddie knew she was bonkers because, as beautiful and charming and popular and rich as she was, her laugh flew in the face of these usually admirable attributes, sounding like it had been dredged up from Hell itself.

Baldy came up behind her. 'You want us to kill him?'

Alison Beech's cold blue eyes swept over Scuttles. She was walking on his grave. 'Yes,' she said. 'But not just yet. I just can't afford another baby-sitter.' Then she cackled again.

'Sure, boss,' said Baldy. Then he turned to Muscles and barked, 'Okay. Get the lorries!'

Muscles immediately raised a walkie-talkie and spoke into it.

In response, from somewhere way on the other side of the warehouse, Eddie heard engines starting.

'They're moving them,' Eddie whispered, reaching into his bag and removing his mum's mobile phone. 'We have to call the police now or we'll lose them.'

The Albino glanced back at him, and for the first time he saw real fear on her face. 'We don't deal with the police,' she said.

'We have to, they're going to get away!'

He squinted at the numbers on the phone then, just as he went to prod the first nine of 999, the Albino grabbed his wrist.

'I said, No police.'

Her grip was strong. He tried to peel her fingers away. 'We need help!'

'I said no peelers.'

Each time he freed one of her fingers, she managed to curl it back around his wrist.

'Then call your gang, get them here if they're so great!'

She looked at the phone for a moment, then shook her head. 'I can't. They're busy.'

'What?' Eddie snapped incredulously. 'Too busy to collect a one million pound reward?'

The Albino shook her head disdainfully. 'You wouldn't understand, we have commitments elsewhere.'

'Well, if your lot won't help, then I'm calling the cops.'

Eddie snapped his wrist out of her grip and quickly jabbed the numbers.

The Albino grabbed for the phone again and managed to catch his hand. He pulled back but she held on and this time began to pry at his fingers which were now gripped tightly around the phone.

'What is *wrong* with you?' Eddie demanded.

'*You are!*' She twisted his little finger backwards, hard. That did the trick. As he jerked his hand away he let go of the phone. It seemed to hang in the air for an eternity. The Albino grabbed for it – and missed. Then they both watched open-mouthed as it fell like a stone – and smashed at Alison Beech's feet far below.

For a moment nobody moved. Not Alison Beech, not Muscles or Baldy or the babies or Eddie or the Albino.

Even when she did react, Alison Beech didn't look up to the roof of the warehouse like any normal person would. She kept her eyes on the shattered phone and said quietly: 'There are uninvited guests at the party. Please find them and kill them.'

Twenty-Seven

Everything seemed to happen at once. An alarm began to wail, the full lights of the warehouse came on immediately above them, a door opened in the far distance and a dozen men came hurrying in. And somebody shouted: 'There they are!'

Fear can work in different ways.

It can freeze you, so you can do nothing.

Or it can galvanise you into action.

It's how people are killed or captured.

It's also how great deeds are accomplished.

Fear and bravery can be the heads and tails of a coin, completely opposite but joined together for ever.

And there was a moment when Eddie couldn't move at all, when all his worst possible fears seemed to have sunk to his feet and hardened there like concrete.

But then, from below, one of the babies cried out, and that snapped him out of it. He *couldn't* be caught, because if he was, something dreadful would happen to him and to the babies, even to the Albino.

She looked as frozen as he was.

Eddie put a hand on her shoulder.

'We can't stay up here,' he said, as calmly as he could.

She looked at him vacantly for a moment, then shook herself, nodded and a moment later she was leading him across the top shelves.

If Eddie's climbing had seemed slow and unsure before, suddenly he was moving with the confidence of a mountain gazelle. He was aware but suddenly unafraid of the rusty shelves, the rotting boxes and the huge drop to the hard concrete below. They had to get down to ground level and lose themselves in the labyrinth of aisles and shelves.

There were more shouts and racing footsteps from far below, threats were hurled through the dusty air, but they ignored them and climbed, turning left at the junction of two stacks of shelves, then right at the next one until they momentarily lost sight of their pursuers. The Albino quickly pointed down and they swung on to a lower shelf, then another and another. Sensing that that was far enough for now, the Albino then led Eddie for another hundred metres along that level, paused to listen, then they swung down lower again. They continued this way for another five minutes, climbing, stopping, listening, swinging down. The alarm had been switched off by now, which somehow made it even more frightening.

Then they heard the bark and growl of dogs being released and the scurried excitement of their soft paws on the hard floor.

Great, Eddie thought, *we're going to be torn limb from limb*.

But the Albino glanced back and she was grinning.

'What're you looking so happy about?' Eddie hissed.

'You ever heard of a dog that could climb?'

He had to admit, she had a point.

They raced further along the shelves, moving more quickly here because the lower levels were tightly packed, making their progress easier. They twisted this way and that until they were lost in the heart of the warehouse and were sure that even if a hundred of Alison Beech's men were searching for them they wouldn't be found.

Eventually the barking of the dogs and the cries of their masters faded away. Perhaps they had found the window with the glass removed and the drugged dog outside and guessed that they had slipped away.

Or perhaps they had been distracted by the three huge lorries now rumbling down the widest of the aisles, making slow, meticulous progress towards the room where the babies were being held.

The babies would be loaded on board and driven away. Eddie had no idea what Alison Beech had planned for them, but he knew she wasn't looking for new homes for them. She wasn't going to buy them presents and love them and care for them.

She was planning something dreadful.

The Albino said nothing, and Eddie said nothing, but they had clearly both come to the same conclusion. Instead of seeking a way out of the warehouse, they found themselves moving back towards the babies.

They ducked down as the lorries rumbled past – only raising their heads a fraction above the boxes, just enough to see Alison Beech's gigantic eyes staring at them from the sides of the vehicles, just enough to read the letters: *Alison Beech International*.

International – maybe that was it, maybe she was going to spirit the babies away to some foreign country where she could do what she planned to do undisturbed.

They had travelled in almost a complete circle, although they were now at a lower level than before. They slithered over the last line of boxes between them and the room below and peered down. They could see that one wall had been completely removed and a lorry had reversed through the gap. The men who had been searching for them were now employed lifting the cots, with the babies inside, and carrying them up a ramp into the back of the lorry. Muscles removed Scuttles' chain from the spike and led him by it up the ramp. Having secured the cots inside the lorry the men moved back down the ramp, loaded it back inside the vehicle then slammed the doors shut, cutting to a dead silence the cries of the babies within. Then they divided themselves between the three lorries. Neither Eddie nor the Albino could see Alison Beech.

As they watched, the lorry with the babies reversed out of the room and into the aisle, taking up a position between the other two vehicles. Then all three began to move forward. The gigantic warehouse doors began to slide open, but because of their width the lorries had to take the same circuitous route to reach them. As soon as they'd moved out of sight, leaving the room below empty, Eddie and the Albino clambered down. They raced across the floor, and peered out just in time to see the lorries veer off to the left. Taking a shortcut along three narrow aisles, Eddie and the Albino emerged on to one of the wider passages that the small convoy of lorries would have to take to reach the doors.

Then they started to climb again.

Just as they reached the first level, the dogs appeared from nowhere, snapping at their heels. One made a tremendous jump and managed to sink its teeth into one of Eddie's trainers, but he was just able to shake it off.

The dogs remained snarling down below as Eddie and the Albino continued their climb, reaching the tenth level and ducking down just as the lorries turned into the aisle and began to snort and rumble down the concrete towards the exit.

'We're not really going to do this, are we?' the Albino whispered.

Eddie shrugged. 'We'll roll off and get crushed.'

'Or torn apart by the dogs.'

'Or caught by Alison Beech and chained up like Scuttles.'

The dogs began to howl excitedly as the lorries approached, jumping up with their paws on the first level of boxes, their sharp teeth pointed up towards the tenth level. But instead of stopping to investigate, the lorries thundered on, blasting their horns to scatter the now confused animals.

The first lorry passed beneath them.

'This is complete madness,' said Eddie.

The second, containing the babies, went by as well.

'We're going to die,' said the Albino.

Eddie took a deep breath. 'Looks like it,' he said.

Then he held out his hand.

The Albino hesitated for a moment, then took it.

Then together they leapt out from the boxes towards the roof of the third lorry.

Twenty-Eight

Eddie and the Albino held on for dear life.

They had landed okay – but getting on wasn't the problem, it was staying on.

They were thrown this way and that as they scrambled towards the front of the third lorry and the theoretical protection of a blind spot behind the driver's cab. The Albino almost slipped off, her feet dangling out over the edge, but Eddie, finally getting a firm grip on a metal bracket on the back of the cab, was able to reach out and haul her back in. Eddie hadn't thought it possible that her face could become any whiter, but now he knew it was. And he didn't look too healthy himself.

They held tight on to the bracket while the lorry twisted its way along the slip road, until finally they were able to relax just a little bit as the convoy joined the much straighter motorway.

'Thank you for saving me,' the Albino panted, avoiding his eyes.

'Don't mention it,' said Eddie. Then added

needlessly: 'Thank you for throwing my phone away.'

'I didn't throw it away!'

'Oh that's right, I forgot, it just jumped by itself. It committed suicide.'

'Oh shut your bake!'

'Aye, right, shut your own bloody cake hole.'

They glared at each other. Then they shivered as the cold wind bit into them. Gradually, and purely for warmth, they drew closer together. The motorway was lit only by the headlights of the lorries, and there was hardly any other traffic. Eddie reckoned it was about three in the morning, and even though it was close to midsummer, when it normally grew light early, there was as yet no hint of an approaching dawn.

They had been travelling in angry silence for about twenty minutes when the Albino finally said, 'Sorry about the phone.'

Eddie supposed that he should apologise as well, although he wasn't sure what for. He just said, 'Sorry too.' She gave him a half smile. They peered forward into the darkness. They had no idea where they were, or where they were going. Sure, they were still close to the babies, but what could they really hope to achieve beyond a horrible death? A few hours from now Barney could be washing their bodies. Eddie shook his head. 'Why wouldn't you let me call the police?'

The Albino shrugged. 'Because.'

'Because what?'

At first he didn't think she was going to respond. She got kind of a faraway look in her eyes. But then she said quietly, 'Because they put my dad in prison.'

'Oh. Right.' He said it as sympathetically as possible, but then couldn't resist asking: 'What for?'

'For something he didn't do.'

'Oh. Right. Why would they do that?'

'Because that's what they do!'

'Are you sure they didn't just make a mis—'

'Of course I'm sure! They said he had a gun! They said he shot someone! He would *never* have a gun! He wouldn't hurt a fly! They set him up! They framed him!'

Andytown and the Rivers were on the news all the time because people were always getting shot. He had kind of thought everyone there had a gun anyway.

'Then why didn't you call your gang?'

'I told you. They're busy. Now will you just shut up and think of a plan?'

'I *already did*.' She was so annoying. '*Two*

plans. The police and your gang. Unfortunately you threw my phone away.'

'I didn't throw it away!'

'Well, I don't hear you coming up with any plans! What's *your* bright idea?'

'I don't have one!'

She turned her back on him then, and for the next ten miles or so as they travelled further and further from the city, deep into the heart of the country, they ignored each other.

Eventually she said: 'This isn't a plan. It's just a statement of fact. We are going *somewhere*, and that *somewhere* will probably be controlled by Alison Beech – so if we're going to do anything we have to do it here, on the open road. We have to find some way of stopping the lorries before—'

'Smoke bombs!' Eddie exclaimed suddenly.

She looked at him like he was barking. 'We don't *have* smoke bombs or any other type of—'

'Yes we bloody do.'

Eddie pulled around his bag with his one free hand and delved inside. He produced three of the small pink tablets his dad had used for smoking out greenfly in the garden. The Albino examined them curiously while he looked back inside his bag for matches.

'Damn,' he said. He had forgotten them! What a tube he was.

'This any use?' the Albino asked. She was holding a lighter.

Eddie nodded, and took it from her. 'Does this mean you smoke?' he asked as he flicked at the lighter. She nodded. 'It'll kill you,' he said.

'And racing down the motorway on the top of a lorry won't?'

Eddie couldn't help but laugh. 'Fair point.' He changed his position slightly to give maximum protection from the wind, then flicked the lighter again. It lit easily.

The important thing now was to cause the lorry with the babies to pull off the road without drawing attention to themselves. They would have to throw the smoke bombs and hope that

(a) they wouldn't miss
(b) if they *did* hit they wouldn't roll off
(c) that the rushing wind wouldn't put out the spark of flame before it had a chance to properly ignite
(d) that they wouldn't fall off the lorry in the act of throwing them
(e) well, actually, there was a whole alphabet of

dangerousness associated with what they were about to attempt, but we have to call a halt somewhere.

They weren't the kind of bombs that exploded – the first one just let out a loud hiss and choking grey smoke began to belch out of it. Eddie couldn't risk standing behind the cab in case the driver looked in his mirror, so with one hand on the metal bracket he leaned out into the wind on the passenger side and threw the bomb towards the lorry ahead.

He had a good strong arm and the bomb hurtled through the air – it struck the roof of the lorry, but then skidded across it and off into the darkness.

Eddie cursed to himself and hauled himself back to light the second bomb. This time it landed right on the cab and stayed there. He was just about to let out a little whoop of triumph when the smoke suddenly died, extinguished by the full force of the wind as it hit the top of the vehicle.

He knelt back down and lit the third and final bomb. As he was about to throw it the Albino stopped him. 'Let me try,' she said.

'But it's our last—'

'I know.'

There was something about the determined look on her face that told him not to argue.

He put the already hissing bomb in her hand, then watched as she gripped the bracket, swung herself out and sliced the missile through the air as if she was merely aiming skimmers out to sea.

The smoke bomb hit the back of the second lorry, bounced once, twice, then slid across the roof and lodged itself directly behind the cab, completely protected from the rush of the wind.

The smoke began to really bellow out until the cab itself was completely obscured. The third lorry, the one they were travelling on, immediately began to honk its horn.

And for half a mile that was it.

Eddie feared that they were so determined to make off with the babies they would pay no attention to the smoke, which was already beginning to fade, and press on regardless. But then the first lorry indicated left and pulled off on to a slip road, quickly followed by the other two vehicles. Up ahead Eddie could see a neon-lit motorway service station surrounded by parked lorries. As they drew closer he could see a shop with a small café attached to it about which several groups of drivers stood talking amongst themselves. Nobody paid much attention as the small convoy came to a halt or as Muscles and Baldy hurried back to examine the second lorry.

What if we just jump up now and start shouting? They'll shoot us down like dogs.

Nothing was said. It was obvious to both of them. They had a problem which would not be solved by jumping up and down. Instead they stayed low and focused their attention on the pay-phone outside the café. All they had to do was get to it without being spotted.

Simple, really.

Twenty-Nine

Muscles and Baldy climbed on to the top of the second lorry, but evidently found nothing. Probably the remnants of the smoke bomb had blown away. They scratched their heads and checked all around the roof and then down the sides. By the time they'd jumped down again to check the engine and the underside of the vehicle, the other drivers and the rest of the gang, some twelve men in all, had gathered in a small group and were talking urgently amongst themselves. Something was said to Baldy and he shook his head, then he turned to Muscles, who shrugged. This was enough for the men, who turned in a group and hurried towards the café. Baldy spoke with Muscles again, then followed them, leaving Muscles to guard the babies.

As the men entered the café, the Albino slipped down on to the tarmac and raced across it, diving beneath the closest of the other lorries. Then, using each one for cover, she was able to quickly scurry across the car park until she was just a few metres from the pay-phone. They had agreed that it was too risky for Eddie to approach the phone – both Muscles and Baldy knew what he looked like. As strange as the Albino looked, and as unusual as it was for a kid to be out and about at such a late hour, at least they wouldn't think to connect her to the stolen babies. After another exchange of angry whispers the Albino had reluctantly conceded that they had no alternative but to phone the police – even if her gang hadn't been tied up elsewhere, they were now too far away to summon for help. Only the police could save the babies now.

The Albino slipped into the phone booth and raised the receiver. You don't need money to phone the police. You just dial 999. But what you do need is a phone that works. And this one didn't. In fact, the receiver wasn't even connected to the phone any more. The Albino stepped out of the booth with the receiver in her hand so that Eddie could clearly see her dilemma.

Eddie signalled for her to return to the lorry. She replaced the receiver and started to walk towards him, but then she stopped suddenly and turned back. She entered the café. He watched horrified as she walked right up to Baldy and started talking.

A thousand panicked thoughts raced through Eddie's head.

And all of them were exactly the same.

She's betraying me!

He could see Baldy reaching into his pocket.

Thirty pieces of silver for selling me down the river!

But no – wait!

She wasn't getting money. She was borrowing his mobile phone!

Baldy was smiling at her and lending her his phone and she was stepping off to one side to make a private phone call – to the police!

Oh, the bravery of the girl!

Oh, the ingenuity!

She even had the nerve to stand by the café window and give a secretive thumbs-up to him across the car park.

Which, after performing such an inspired act of bravery, was probably the stupidest thing she'd done in her life.

Because Baldy was watching her and, even though she'd hidden her hand signal, he followed her gaze across the car park and just caught the merest glimpse of Eddie on top of the third lorry.

The Albino saw Baldy suddenly jump up out of his seat.

She dropped the phone and ran for the door.

Baldy yelled and charged after her. The gangsters jumped to follow, but there were other, ordinary drivers in their way. The Albino had just a few seconds to grab an umbrella that was hanging on a stand near the swing doors. She burst through them, then turned and pushed the umbrella through the handles, jamming them shut.

At least temporarily.

Baldy crashed against them a moment later, but the umbrella held. It was a good umbrella.

There was no time for hiding now.

The Albino dashed across the tarmac.

Muscles had already heard the commotion and came round from checking behind the lorries to confront her.

He had probably never seen such a vision before – this porcelain girl racing towards him with her eyes wide and angry.

'Out of my way you stupid big fat eejit!' she screamed.

And Muscles, despite being four times the size of her, took a step back, confused, as if someone was playing a trick on him.

Then he looked back towards the café where he could see Baldy and the rest of the gang hammering on the glass doors and he knew that this was serious.

But he had taken a step back too far. Eddie hurled himself from the top of the third lorry and landed on top of Muscles. The big man staggered forward as Eddie closed his arms around his head and twisted hard. Muscles yelled – but he didn't let go. He began to twirl Eddie around his head, trying to shake him off. Eddie held tight and began to pummel Muscles' head and throat with his fists, but he just wasn't strong enough to stop him.

'Kiiiiicckkkhimmmminnnnntheeeeewilllllllllly . . .' Eddie screamed as he was spun round and round.

It took several moments for the Albino to understand what Eddie was yelling about, but then the penny dropped and she launched herself forward. She punched Muscles once in the willy, which stopped him in his tracks. Then she kicked him hard, which dropped him to his knees, rigid with shock and pain. A second kick in exactly the same position saw him keel over. Eddie tumbled from his shoulders, but rolled expertly and was immediately back on his feet. As Muscles lay gasping for air, the Albino leaned over him and slipped the keys to the lorry out of his jacket pocket.

Fifty metres away across the tarmac the glass doors of the café shattered and the gang stumbled angrily out.

Eddie followed the Albino across to the second lorry and climbed up into the cab. She immediately slipped the keys into the ignition and started the engine.

Eddie stared at her. 'What are you doing?' he shouted. 'You can't drive this!'

She laughed suddenly back at him. 'Why not? I'm an Andytown Albino! We can do anything!'

And with that she threw the lorry into gear, spun the steering wheel to the left, reached to the very tip of her toes to press the accelerator, and thundered out of the car park, leaving the despairing Baldy, the groaning Muscles and the rest of the gang trailing in her wake.

Thirty

Bernard J. Scuttles – Head of Security at the Royal Victoria Hospital, guardian of twelve helpless babies, kidnap victim facing certain death – had reached the end of his tether. His position had been grim to start with, but for the past twenty minutes he had been thrown this way and that in the back of the lorry; convinced it was being driven by a madman, and that it would soon crash and kill them all. It had lurched to one side then another, hurling him against the metal walls and throwing several of the cots precariously up on to their sides, almost throwing the babies out. When he tried to calm them down, they rewarded him with showers of pee and avalanches of poo, with fountains of vomit and atomic farts which would have had any normal man crying for rescue.

In fact, Scuttles had been rescued.

He just didn't realise it.

When the lorry finally came to a halt, Scuttles had a damp nappy stuck to the side of his face and one shoe filled with warm milk. This was no way for a man to die, he told himself. It was time to go out fighting.

He vowed to launch an assault on his kidnappers the instant the lorry doors opened. He would battle through them and escape, or he would perish in the attempt.

But what he needed was a weapon. He searched the back of the lorry. As he checked the cots he found that one had cracked down the side. He was able to lift the baby out and slip it in with one of the others. They immediately snuggled together for warmth. Then Scuttles snapped off two legs. The legs of the cot – not of the babies. That would have been cruel. The cot legs were made of a hard, dark wood, and were excellent for hitting people with.

Thus, when the door of the lorry was finally pulled open, Scuttles gave a huge war cry, ready to launch himself at and bash the brains in of whoever was standing there.

Like the two kids staring at him.

Like that brat Eddie Malone.

Like the ghost beside him.

Eddie and the Albino jumped back with a shout. Scuttles only just stopped himself from whacking them.

He kept his clubs up high in case the kids were trying to lull him into a false sense of security; he stared around at his new surroundings: the lorry was now sitting in a cavernous barn, there was straw everywhere, a few chickens were strutting about – but there was no sign of the kidnappers, no sign of Alison Beech.

'What the hell are you doing here? What the hell is going on? Where are the—'

'Shut your fridge, Scuttles,' Eddie snapped.

He felt good. Excited. Confident. They had led the baby-snatchers' lorries on a wild chase, first along the motorway, and then along narrow and twisting country roads. The Albino wasn't the best driver in the world, but she was fearless. She raced around corners at top speed on the wrong side of the road not even bothering to think what might be coming in the opposite direction. She squeezed through gaps in hedges huge lorries were not supposed to squeeze through. She jumped ditches as if she was on a horse. And she drove with the pedal to the metal through thick fog when she couldn't see more than a few metres in front of her, not paying a blind bit of attention to Eddie screaming at her to slow down.

It was the fog that had saved them.

For, as fearless as she was, the chasing drivers were just as good, following her through every twist and turn. But with the descent of the fog, she was able finally to give them the slip, rolling across several fields before coming across this largely empty barn.

All they had to do was wait for the fog to lift, then seek help.

And deal with Scuttles.

'Don't you tell me to—' Scuttles began.

'We'll tell you whatever we feel like,' the Albino snapped, 'because we saved your arse.' Scuttles thought about that for a moment, and had to concede that they probably had. 'That means you owe us, big time.'

'I don't owe . . . I . . . I . . . I . . . couldn't . . . you . . . what do you *mean* you saved me? How? Why?'

'How? Because we outfoxed them.'

'Why?' said Eddie. 'Well we saved the babies because we had to. We saved you by accident. But we still did it.'

The only way Scuttles could deal with it, the fact that two punk kids had rescued him from certain death, was to ignore it. 'We need to get the babies home,' he said. 'They need feeding, whichever one of you was driving, their milk is all over the place. They're hungry.'

And they were. Each and every one of them was screaming to be fed.

'That may be,' said Eddie, 'but first I need you to swear to God.'

'Swear *what* to God?'

'That you'll never go out with my mother again.'

The Albino was looking at him oddly. But Eddie was determined. It was probably the only opportunity he would ever have to get one over on Bernard J. Scuttles.

'Fair enough,' said Scuttles.

'And I want my laptop back.'

'Okay.'

'And two new bikes.'

'Don't push it, kid.'

They glared at each other until the Albino stepped between them. 'As soon as the fog lifts and the coast is clear, we'll go for help. But in the meantime' – she looked into the back of the lorry – 'we've got work to do.'

And they had.

They were able to rescue some of the spilled baby milk powder from the lorry floor and then drain boiling water from the engine in order to mix up the formula. They had enough bottles, but not enough hands; even when they each held a baby in the crook of each arm, that still left six gasping to be fed. There weren't enough nappies to go around so they had to make do with washing those that had merely been peed in in a barrel just inside the barn door. They then dried them by switching the cab's heater on full blast and draping the damp nappies over the seats.

However, it seemed that the harder they worked to satisfy the babies, the less appreciated it was. They cried and they cried and they cried.

And they cried and they cried and they cried.

And they cried and they cried and they cried until it threatened to drive them all mad.

Eddie, the Albino and Scuttles slumped down, exhausted, close to defeat, covered in milk powder and little spits of sick, with their ears ringing and their throats ragged from *shhhhing* the babies over and over again.

Just when they thought they couldn't take any more, when the sensible option seemed to be just to phone up the baby-snatchers and say here, have them back, because we can't take any more, just as they reached that very point, Scuttles started to sing.

Eddie had no idea what song it was, but it sounded old and Irish and, even though it was Scuttles singing, soft and beautiful and haunting. Gradually, one by one, they stopped crying. Then they gurgled contentedly. And, before the song was finished, all of the babies had fallen fast asleep.

Eddie nearly went over himself. The Albino had to pinch herself. She said, 'That was lovely,' and yawned.

Scuttles shrugged, and gave a half smile.

They sat and enjoyed the silence, lost in their own thoughts. The damp air of the night had given way to the drier heat of early summer. Scuttles looked around the barn and turned up a ripped and paint-splattered pair of old trousers, which he quickly pulled on over his underpants, then gave a long sigh of relief. A man can endure horrific experiences and unpleasant tortures without batting an eyelid, but few can face running around in just their underpants for very long. Especially when they're grey and baggy and very slightly smelly. The underpants, that is. Now he felt like a human being again. Eddie and the Albino felt better about it as well. They were sick and tired of looking at his baggy bum poking through his Y-fronts.

The Albino rescued half a dozen eggs from the hens that strutted at will around the barn and divided them up. Eddie looked at his, lost as to what to do with them.

'What we need,' he said, 'is a microwave.'

'Yeah right,' said the Albino, and cracked one on the side of the van. She drank down the yoke with relish, threw the shell behind her, then wiped the back of her hand across her sticky mouth.

'Don't you know about eating raw eggs?' Eddie said. 'Now you're going to die a horrible death.'

'You don't want yours then?' She put her hand out to take them back.

Eddie looked at them. He *was* starving. Beside him Scuttles cracked two eggs at once and drank them down. 'Lovely,' he said.

Eddie took a deep breath. He cracked one egg, raised it to his mouth, closed his eyes and drank it down.

At least if they were going to die, they would all die together.

Apart from the vomiting, they suffered no ill effects.

Scuttles held the Albino's hand while she threw up. Eddie went off into a corner and was sick there.

Scuttles just heaved into a corner like it was the most natural thing in the world.

As the Albino tried to recover her balance, and her dignity, Scuttles reached over to smooth her sweaty hair down, but she bent away out of his reach. Holding her hand was one thing, but this was clearly a step too far. His hand hovered awkwardly in the air for several moments, then he withdrew it. Eddie didn't think she had a problem with Scuttles himself, just that she wasn't used to being helped in this way. But Scuttles wasn't easily put off, he was determined to strike up a relationship. 'So,' he said, 'what's your name and how did you end up with buggerlugs here?'

Buggerlugs was even worse than Curly, but Eddie was too tired and sick to protest.

The Albino looked at Eddie. 'My name is Mary Agnes Caitlin Delores Assumpta O'Riorden. But my friends call me Mo. And we ended up together by accident.'

'Well, Mo, you seem to make a pretty good team.'

She shrugged. 'We do okay.' She kept her eyes on Eddie, who didn't look back. Instead he nodded at the barn doors.

'Why don't you check if the fog has lifted yet, Mary?' Eddie said.

She looked surprised, and a little bit hurt that he had chosen not to use her preferred name. She climbed to her feet and stomped across to where a plank had previously been wrenched out of the barn door. He didn't quite know why he was being mean to her. He just was.

Scuttles tutted and shook his head at Eddie, who sat where he was with his arms folded. 'Eddie, why don't you—?'

'Why don't you mind your own business?' Eddie snapped.

Scuttles shook his head, then went to check on the babies. Eddie watched Mo at the door for several moments, then sighed. He went over to her.

She was aware of him behind her, but she didn't look round.

'Sorry,' he said. She didn't respond. 'This is just all so crazy, I'm just all . . .'

'The fog's gone,' she said. 'There's nothing moving in the field or on the road. But that doesn't mean they're not out there. We should stay here as long as we can. They'll stop searching soon. They have to.'

She turned and walked back to the lorry without looking at him. She climbed up into the cab. Eddie followed. Mo turned the key in the ignition far enough to give them power, then switched on the radio. Predictably, all of the news channels they could pick up were talking about the missing babies. As they listened, Scuttles joined them in the cab, his face growing progressively greyer as he listened.

'Police are renewing their appeal for information which might lead to the arrest of Bernard J. Scuttles, the former Head of Security at the Royal Victoria Hospital . . .'

'*Former* Head . . . ?' Scuttles spluttered. 'Arrest . . . ?'

'Shhhh,' said Mo, 'listen.'

'Mr Scuttles is thought to have provided the security codes which allowed the baby-snatchers access to the hospital's maternity wing.'

'I never did!' Scuttles groaned.

'*Shhhhhh!*' said Eddie.

'He is thought to be armed and highly dangerous and should not be approached.'

'Me? I'm about as dangerous as a pint of custard!'

Scuttles buried his face in his hands.

'Police are also increasingly concerned about the disappearance of a known associate of Bernard Scuttles. Twelve-year-old Edward Malone vanished from his home in the grounds of the

Royal Victoria Hospital late last night. At this point police are not commenting on whether he is involved in the kidnappings, or has become another victim.'

'Edward Malone's mother was too upset to speak to waiting reporters, but his father had this to say:

His father!

His father had rushed home or they had tracked him down wherever he was living with Spaghetti Legs.

His dad!

He wanted to hold him and hug him and explain.

He knew of all people that his dad would understand.

That his dad would defend him, support him, rescue him even.

Eddie felt like crying. And after he heard his father's words he felt even more like crying.

'Eddie is a good boy, and I'm sure there's a perfectly innocent explanation. I know he wouldn't want to upset his mum like this. Please come home, Eddie, we can work this out.'

He felt even more like crying because it wasn't his father's voice.

It was Baldy's.

Thirty-One

'Blackmail, that's what you call it. You do what they say, or they'll do something unspeakably horrible to your mum. To my girlfriend.'

'She's not your bloody girl – you promised!'

'Eddie, that's not the point right now.'

'Well, what is?!'

Eddie wheeled away from Scuttles, a weird mix of horror and anger on his face. His mum was in the clutches of Baldy and Muscles, and behind them was Alison Beech, the woman she admired above all others.

'The choice,' Scuttles said, as sympathetically as he could, 'is whether to take the babies back to them, and save your mum, or give them to the police and doom her to—'

'Will you shut your door!' Eddie yelled. 'Just . . . *be quiet*. I have to think.'

He walked across the barn and sat down on an old milking stool.

Mum . . . the babies . . . Mum . . . the babies . . . Mum . . .

The problem was, there was no right thing to do.

Every solution had its down side; and every down side had its solution.

He couldn't just give the twelve babies to Alison Beech.

And he couldn't sacrifice his mum.

If only he could be in two places at the same time. Hand the babies to the police, and rescue his mum at the same time.

If only there was someone he could call on to help. Some friend or . . .

Some gang.

Eddie stood abruptly. 'Mary . . . Mo,' he said, 'I need your help.'

Mo, who could see how upset he was, nodded.

'I need the Andytown Albinos to find my mum and rescue her.'

'That's not possible,' she said quickly. 'I wish it was.'

'Why not?'

'Because.'

'Because isn't good enough any more! Why not?!'

'I don't . . . I don't wield that sort of power with them, I can't just—'

'My mother is going to die! Or these babies are!

You can't just say no! You have to help!'

But she shook her head.

'What sort of a gang would allow twelve little babies to die, Mo, when it's within their power to save them?'

Mo bit her lip and averted her eyes.

'I'll tell you what sort of a gang,' Scuttles said.

'What would *you* know about it?' Eddie demanded sharply.

'It's part of my job to know. I meet with the police every month to discuss security at the hospital, and they tell me what the various gangs are up to, what to watch out for. So I know all about the Andytown Albinos.'

He nodded across at Mo.

'Don't,' she said.

'Then you tell him. Go on, tell him all about the Andytown Albinos.'

Mo folded her arms and stared at the ground.

'What is it, Mo?' Eddie asked. She wouldn't look at him, and she wouldn't reply. He turned to Scuttles. 'What's the big deal?'

'The big deal? Well, it's actually a small deal, isn't it, Mo?' Again she didn't respond. 'Because the fact of the matter is – there *is* no Andytown Albinos. There is no gang. The Andytown Albinos are one little girl who causes a hell of a lot of trouble. It is you, isn't it? It just took me a while to figure it out, when it should have been obvious. The police have been after you for ages.'

Mo certainly wasn't denying it. She tilted her head up slightly towards Eddie. 'I'm sorry,' she said.

Eddie surprised her by laughing. 'Sorry? Mo – what have you got to be sorry about? The Reservoir Pups are scared witless of the Andytown Albinos, they think you're like this huge army of thugs. I was with about fifty of them and they wouldn't put one foot inside your territory. If you're the Andytown Albinos, just you, then what you've achieved is – awesome. Incredible!'

'You think so?'

'Of course! I just don't know how you managed it.'

Mo shrugged. 'I work at night, in the dark. People are scared of things they can't see. And when they tell someone else about it, they always exaggerate. I haven't done half the damage people say I have.'

'You've done enough!' said Scuttles. 'You're a menace to society! You should be locked up.'

Eddie snapped. 'She *rescued* you, you ungrateful, fat pig!'

Scuttles looked rather hurt. 'I'm not fat,' he said, 'I'm big-boned.' Then he stalked off towards the lorry. One of the babies was crying again.

As he hauled himself up inside the lorry, Mo said, 'But it means I can't help rescue your mum, Eddie. I have no soldiers, there's just me.'

'And you're enough,' said Eddie, suddenly enthusiastic again, 'because if the Pups don't know, that means we can make a deal with them. You offer them something – territory or a percentage of some deal or part of the reward – and then *they'll* rescue my mum.'

'Do you think so?'

'I *know* so. All we have to do is make contact, get to a phone, let me do the—'

Suddenly, the lorry started up behind them.

They turned to see Scuttles in the driver's seat and for a moment they feared he was going to take off with the babies. But instead he wound down his window. 'I may be fat, but I still know the difference between right and wrong. And she's as much bloody trouble as you are. But the decision about your mum has been taken out of your hands. One of the babies is sick, really sick. We need to go for help.'

'But my mum—'

'Either get on board now, or I'm taking them out of here by myself.'

'But they could be waiting out there!' Mo shouted.

'Well, that's a risk we have to take. Now, are you coming or not?'

Mo looked at Eddie, and Eddie looked back. Then they nodded simultaneously and climbed up. They couldn't let the baby die, that was obvious. But neither were they going to abandon his mum. They would work something out.

Seconds later the lorry smashed through the doors of the barn, sending splinters of wood shooting high into the air.

'You didn't have to destroy the doors,' Eddie said, as they raced across the field towards the road.

'I know,' Scuttles said with a grin, 'but it was fun, wasn't it?'

Thirty-Two

The baby was clearly unwell. Its skin was blotchy and damp to the touch, and every time it took a rest from screaming, it threw up. They had to get it to a doctor. They had to deliver the other babies to the police. They had to rescue Eddie's mum. They had to make a deal with the Reservoir Pups. They had to do a lot of things and they couldn't do them all at the same time.

The natural thing to do, if they had all been the best of friends, would have been to split up – Eddie make the call to the Pups, Mo take the baby to the nearest doctor, Scuttles deliver the rest to the police station. But as they really didn't trust each other quite yet, none of them would agree to dividing their tasks up like this. Eddie worried that Scuttles would claim the reward money for himself. Mo thought that Eddie would give too much away to the Reservoir Pups in exchange for their help. And although Scuttles now appreciated that Eddie and Mo had rescued him from the baby-snatchers, they were still gangsters in miniature and liable to betray him at any moment. So they reached a compromise. Eddie and Mo would make the call to the Pups while Scuttles looked after the babies in the lorry; Eddie would hold the keys to the lorry so that Scuttles wouldn't drive off. Then they would all drive to the police station, where a doctor could be summoned for the sick baby.

They drove without incident to the nearest village, which was called Crossmaheart. Eddie recognised its name from the news and knew that it had seen a lot of trouble in its time, but it seemed all quiet now. There was a Spar shop at one end, with a call box outside, and a small police station, which showed the marks of many bullet holes, at the other.

Eddie took the keys to the lorry and walked across to the phone box with Mo. Scuttles nestled the sick baby in his arms and kissed it on the forehead. It had settled down a little bit in the past ten minutes. Maybe the worst of its sickness had passed, but you couldn't play too safe with little babies, Scuttles knew that from working in the hospital. That and having six younger brothers.

Of course the moment Eddie entered the phone box he realised he didn't have a number for the Reservoir Pups. They were a gang after all, up to all kinds of criminal mischief. They were hardly likely to advertise themselves in the Yellow Pages.

He looked stupidly at Mo. 'I have no way of contacting them.'

Mo lifted the phone and called Directory Enquiries. She asked for the number for the Reservoir Pups.

Eddie was in the act of saying, 'Don't be ridicul—' when Mo said, 'Thank you,' and cut the line. Then she started to punch in a fresh set of numbers. She smiled at Eddie. 'Criminal gangs run legitimate enterprises as cover. They're listed under *Reservoir Pups, Surveillance, Investigation and Demolition.*'

As she waited for someone to answer the phone, Eddie said: 'So what's the Andytown Albinos cover?'

'There are no Andytown Albinos, remember?' Before he could respond, Mo stiffened and quickly handed him the phone.

Eddie took a deep breath.

A voice at the other end said, 'Reservoir Pups – which service please?'

'I need to speak to Captain Black. This is Eddie Malone. It's an emergency.'

'Eddie Malone? Didn't we throw you out a few—'

'It's about the stolen babies!'

'It is you, isn't it? We sold your bike for thirty quid. Could have got more but we—'

'Please!'

'Oh, hold on.'

There was thirty seconds of silence, then a familiar voice said, 'Black.'

'Captain Black . . . this is Eddie Malone. I need your help.'

'Mmmm-hmmm?'

'We . . . I have the stolen babies. I want to give them to the police. But the baby-snatchers have kidnapped my mum. I need you to save her.'

'Need . . . want . . . the important word, I think, is *why*. Why should we help you?'

'Because they're going to kill her if we don't deliver the babies to them.'

'That's not what I asked.'

'Please!'

'What's in it for us?'

Eddie glanced at Mo, who was standing right up close beside him, listening in. She nodded, giving him permission to deal on her behalf.

'I can deliver the Andytown Albinos.'

There was a long pause, and then: 'What do you mean, *deliver*?'

'An undertaking from them not to break the peace agreement again. And a guarantee of safe passage for your people through Albino territory.'

There was a long pause, then Black said coolly: 'It's not enough.'

'Okay – okay,' Eddie said, growing more desperate. 'We . . . she . . . the Andytown Albinos are also willing to give up the industrial estate.'

'Why would they want to do that?'

'Because they care about the babies.'

Black thought about that for another long moment. 'And you can guarantee this?'

'Yes!'

'It's still not enough.'

'What do you want, blood?!'

'Money.'

'We don't have any mon—

'We want half of the reward money. Half a million pounds.'

Eddie's mind was racing. There wasn't going to be any reward money. Alison Beech had offered it, but now that she was about to be unmasked as the chief baby-snatcher she was hardly going to reward them for it as well. But the Reservoir Pups weren't aware of that – so they obviously weren't as all-knowing as they let on. Now it was just a question of being clever with his words. Eddie covered the telephone receiver and pretended that he was talking to someone. After a minute he removed his hand from the speaker and said: 'Okay. They agree to giving you half of whatever they receive.'

There was a lengthy pause, and then Captain Black said: 'Okay. But I warn you, if they fail to deliver, once we've destroyed them, we'll come looking for you.'

'That's fine! Do we have a deal?'

'Yes, Eddie. We have a deal.'

'Brilliant!' Eddie gave Mo the thumbs-up. She nodded. 'My mum, she—'

'We know where she is,' said Black.

'But how, I've only just—'

'Eddie. When are you going to learn? I've told you, nothing happens in our territory we don't know about. They've taken her to the hospital. They're holding her in the secure wing, where they keep all the crazies.'

'The ... My God. You have to get her out of there!' And then he had a sudden brain-wave. 'The security codes! They're in my laptop! If you can get to Scuttles' desk we—'

'We have the security codes, Eddie. We had them all along.'

'But then why did you make me . . . ?'

'Because we wanted to see if you could do it. But you failed. Now, if you want us to rescue your mum, we'd better get on with it.' He hesitated for a moment, then added: 'And look after those babies.'

Then he put the phone down.

Eddie held the receiver in his hand for a moment. He'd done it. Brokered a deal that would allow his mum to be rescued and the babies to be delivered to the police without fear. He smiled widely. Mo smiled back. They almost gave each other a hug – but they held back for a moment too long, and then it felt awkward. They were saved from further embarrassment by Scuttles hammering on the window of his cab and gesturing at them to hurry up. Eddie and Mo looked at each other for a single moment, then hurried out of the call box and climbed back onboard the lorry.

Everything was going to be okay.

These are, of course, known as famous last words because invariably as soon as they are uttered, something awful happens. When someone stands on an icy pond and declares it safe, he generally then plunges through the ice and drowns. It happens during battle when someone stands up and says the enemy couldn't hit a barn door at this range, and then gets shot through the head. And it happens without fail whenever Eddie thinks everything is going to be okay.

They drove along the main street and came to a halt outside the police station. Although this part of the country had known trouble and violence for many years, it was now relatively safe, safe enough for the police garrison to have been reduced to one rather portly officer, who was at that moment half-way up a ladder cleaning the station windows. He didn't hear the lorry, which had a loud, bucolic diesel engine. When it was switched off, he couldn't hear the babies, who were now crying at great volume. And when he finally noticed Scuttles, with the sick baby in his arms, and Eddie and Mo on either side of him, he just nodded pleasantly at them and said good morning and what a lovely day it is, whereas most people, and all police officers, would surely at the very least have recognised the face of possibly the most wanted man in the whole country.

The baby in Scuttles' arms let out another cry. The police officer climbed down his ladder. He beamed down at the baby. 'Oh . . . diddums . . . what's wrong with you, then?'

'He's sick,' Eddie said.

'And we've eleven more just like him,' said Scuttles. 'I think they've caught something.'

The police officer tutted. 'Well, that's just dreadful. The doctor's is just—' And then something finally twigged with him. 'Eleven you say . . . plus one . . . why, that's a dozen.' He fixed Scuttles with his version of an investigative gaze. 'And would you be the father of these—'

'No!' Scuttles exploded. 'These are the babies I have been wrongly accused of stealing! I'm returning them and giving myself up. I know who really did take them and when I tell you it will blow your socks off. Now, please help me get them out of the lorry.'

The police officer looked at Scuttles, then at Eddie – plainly he now recognised him as well – and finally at the ghostly Mo. Suddenly realising that he was on the verge of solving the crime of the century, and completely overwhelmed by this fact, he took a step back and stammered: 'I . . . I . . . I . . . have to make . . . a phone call.'

Scuttles rolled his eyes. 'Just help me get them

out and then phone whoever you want! We promise not to bite.'

'Well . . . well . . . if you say so . . .'

He followed Scuttles back to the lorry as if he was the hired help, and helped them carry the babies in their cots into the police station. He led them down a corridor to the warmest room in the station.

'We need nappies,' Eddie said.

'And milk,' added Mo.

'We need a doctor, two probably – and nurses,' said Scuttles.

'Absolutely,' said the constable. Then he showed them to a small interview room. 'If you would just . . . wouldn't mind waiting . . . in here.' Scuttles fixed him with a steady gaze. 'Please . . .' said the constable, with a vague hint of desperation. Scuttles gave a short sigh, nodded at Eddie and Mo, then all three of them stepped into the interview room.

Immediately the constable grabbed the handle and slammed the door shut. Then he locked it. Bolted it. Double-bolted it. Then he clapped his hands together triumphantly and went to call for help.

Thirty-Three

Of course, it wasn't entirely unexpected, them being locked up. Scuttles was the chief suspect in the baby-snatching. Eddie was thought to be involved. And Mo looked so weird, she was bound to be part of it as well.

So they sat on three of the four chairs that surrounded a cigarette-scarred table and waited to be questioned. One hour went past. Then two. Eddie couldn't help but wonder what the Reservoir Pups were up to. If they had worked out a plan yet for rescuing his mother. Or if they were to be trusted at all. He had no fears about the police. Once they knew who was really behind the baby-snatching, why, they'd be hailed as heroes. Of course, there was no longer any prospect of getting the reward Alison Beech had been offering – but there was bound to be something. And then there would be television appearances. A book – *How I Saved The Babies*, by Eddie Malone. Perhaps a movie. Maybe he could star in it himself.

Scuttles stood up and began to pace back and forth.

He had more to worry about than either Eddie or Mo. If they believed he was the mastermind behind the baby-snatching, then naturally he would try and squirm out of it by blaming someone else. But by pinning it on Alison Beech, they'd not only think he was lying, they'd think he was mad as well. Someone as beautiful, as magnificent, as generous and charitable as Alison Beech? Why, such a suggestion was monstrous.

To help calm his fears, Eddie pulled out the video camera from his bag and showed Scuttles what he had taped from his position high in the warehouse. The picture wasn't perfect – it was dark and Alison Beech had been some considerable distance away – but it was definitely her. A blind man in a coal mine would have recognised her.

'See?' Eddie said. 'Nothing to worry about.'

Scuttles lowered himself wearily into one of the chairs. 'I hope you're right. I can't take much more of this.'

At which point the bolts on the cell door were drawn back and a key turned in the door. Mo looked nervously across as three policemen entered the interview room. Their faces were very serious indeed.

But for Eddie the relief was tremendous. He couldn't help but jump up from his seat to greet the police ecstatically. When he opened his mouth it was as if a river had suddenly burst its banks. 'We saved them!' he bellowed. 'We saved the babies! It's Alison Beech! We have her on tape! She stole them! She was going to do something dreadful with them but we broke into the warehouse! And then we jumped on the back of the lorry! And then we stole them back! I know you think we're criminals but we're not, we got them back!'

Eddie wasn't sure what reaction to expect. Part of him had hoped that he would be carried shoulder high from the station to be greeted by cheering crowds outside. But the police officers merely nodded wisely. One of them said: 'If you'll just come this way, I'm sure we can sort it all out.'

Okay, so they weren't overly excited.

That was understandable. They didn't know all the facts yet. They had to be impartial. They probably wouldn't carry him shoulder high until much later on.

The police indicated for Eddie, Mo and Scuttles

to follow them out of the interview room, then led them down the corridor towards the front door of the station. Eddie led the way, but managed to wink excitedly back at Mo. As they passed the front desk the constable who'd locked them up in the first place could be seen bent over some paperwork, while a second officer, of much higher rank, stood before him, with his back to Eddie and the others as they passed.

Eddie didn't know why he chose that moment to look at the second police officer's shoes. There was just something about them that seemed to invite his attention. Perhaps it was because they weren't shoes at all, but boots. Cowboy boots. Snakeskin cowboy boots.

Eddie stopped suddenly, causing Mo to bump into him.

Just at that moment the police constable behind the desk held up the paperwork. 'I just don't understand this,' he said, shaking his head.

'Well then, perhaps you'll understand this.'

And the Cowboy, for it was he, dressed in a fake police uniform, took out a gun and pointed it across the desk. Simultaneously the other police officers drew their guns and pointed them at Eddie, Mo and Scuttles.

'Now, get down on the floor!' the Cowboy shouted at the constable, who dropped like a stone. Then the Cowboy turned and smiled at Scuttles. 'Bernard,' he said, 'what a pleasure to see you.'

Even though Eddie had already told Scuttles about the Cowboy, he clearly hadn't believed him, because his mouth dropped open and he stammered: 'Vince . . . Vince . . . Vince . . . I don't . . . Vince . . . what are you . . . how did you . . . ?'

The Cowboy laughed. 'It's amazing what you get if you spread a bit of money around, isn't it?' He ordered Eddie, Mo and Scuttles out of the station. Just as they reached the door Eddie glanced back to see the Cowboy standing over the police constable on the floor. He raised his gun. His finger curled around the trigger. The constable squeezed his eyes shut and flattened himself as much as he could against the bare wooden floor.

'BANG,' said the Cowboy, and everyone jumped. The Cowboy laughed again. The constable opened his eyes a fraction, surprised to be alive. He was now visibly shaking, and there were tears rolling down his cheeks. 'You call for help within the hour,' the Cowboy hissed, 'and I'll snap the spines of every single one of those babies, you understand?'

The constable nodded and squeezed his eyes tight shut again.

They travelled south, the gang now changed out of their police uniforms and the babies transferred to a green lorry with *Larry Holmes Meat Products* etched on the side. Eddie, Mo and Scuttles were handcuffed in the back of a much smaller van, which led the way. From time to time the Cowboy, in the van's passenger seat, glanced back at them and shook his head.

'Those babies need a doctor,' Eddie shouted forward, more than once.

'They need feeding,' said Mo. 'They need changing.'

The Cowboy ignored them. Scuttles looked shell-shocked, and sat with his head bowed, muttering away to himself. Eddie felt sorry for him. He'd been betrayed by a trusted colleague. He stopped feeling sorry for him right about the time Scuttles said, 'I just can't believe it, Vince, my mate Vince, behind it all the time. He's been my mate for years. He came to my wedding.'

'Your wedding?' Eddie snapped, forgetting for a moment that he was almost certain to die a horrible death in the near future. 'You're bloody *married*?'

'Well . . .' said Scuttles, scrambling to cover his tracks, 'I . . . I . . . what does it matter now? We're all going to—'

'It matters to me,' said Eddie. 'It *matters* to my mum.'

Mo would have placed a hand on his shoulder to calm him down, but she was handcuffed as well. 'Never mind about him,' she whispered, 'what are *we* going to do?'

Eddie glared at Scuttles for another few moments, then turned to Mo. 'I don't know.' He peered forwards, between the Cowboy and the hood driving the van. Ahead of them now, and beginning to dominate the entire horizon, rose the dark, menacing outline of the Mourne Mountains. In their very centre, glowering down on the peaks around it, stood Slieve Donard. Its lower slopes were blanketed in thunder clouds, lightning crackled above the vast banks of pine and jagged cliffs which guarded its every approach. It did not look to Eddie like a place where anything good ever happened.

And he was quite right.

Thirty-Four

Alison Beech liked to think she was close to nature. Certainly her products – her creams and lotions and oils and sprays – were promoted and sold as if they had been created by Mother Nature herself. In fact, Alison Beech wouldn't know nature if nature came up and slapped her in the face. Her products were actually created by teams of scientists working deep underground with some of the most dangerous, noxious, poisonous chemicals and gases known to man. You may wonder how anything made with dangerous, noxious or poisonous ingredients could ever be sold to the public as something that could make you feel better, smell nicer and look younger, but anything can be dressed up to make it look better than it actually is. Cigarettes, for example – although it has been many years since anybody tried to claim that they were actually good for you – or the humble chocolate éclair, stuffed with fresh cream. One in itself is not bad for you, neither is two or three. But if you eat half a dozen every day for ten years, then almost certainly, one day, when walking down the street, you will simply explode. The same is true of Alison Beech's lotions and potions, superficially good for you, but ultimately extremely dangerous. Of course she hid this fact rather well. Her scientists had to swear to keep it secret, or they'd come to a sticky end, rather like the people who used her products. As for the authorities – well authorities are often . . . How can we say this politely? . . . extremely stupid. If Alison Beech says something is good for you, then her word is certainly good enough. And then, of course, there is the question of money. Alison Beech is a powerful industrial figure, in a country not known for having powerful industrial figures. She employs so many people, and makes so much money, that if the authorities sought to even question the safety of her products she wouldn't hesitate to close down her factories, thousands would become unemployed and the entire economy might collapse. And as if all of that isn't enough, because she has so much money, she can afford to bribe, frighten or simply murder anyone who gets in her way. So you can see that when Alison Beech wants something, she gets it. For example, when she proposed building a giant chemical factory in the shadow of the Mourne Mountains there was an international outcry. Presidents, prime ministers and pop stars demanded that such an area of outstanding natural beauty be left alone, but under her intense gaze, the authorities caved in – almost literally. They allowed her to build her massive stinking chemical factory *inside* Slieve Donard. They tore up the rule-book, and the laws of nature, and gave her permission to hollow out a mountain.

You wouldn't even know it was there.

Unless you drove straight at the side of that mountain and, instead of crashing into it, you stumbled upon a road so brilliantly camouflaged that you could be forgiven for thinking that the vast banks of pine trees had actually slid apart to allow you to enter the dark interior.

And so they entered the mountain.

They were waved through a security checkpoint and then drove along a tunnel which was wide enough to allow traffic in both directions. After a few minutes it began to twist into a kind of stretched spiral which led them deeper and deeper into the core of the mountain. Eventually it flattened out again as it reached the floor of a cavernous hall that had clearly been blasted and sucked from the once mighty innards of Slieve Donard. Eddie felt somehow heavier down here, like someone had suddenly dropped a shroud weighed down with lead pebbles over his head and shoulders. And it smelled like – for a moment he couldn't put his finger on it. And then it came to him. It smelled like the room in the hospital where his friend washed the dead bodies.

The van came to a halt, with the lorry beside it. Eddie, Mo and Scuttles were bundled out and made to stand under guard while the cots were collected by squads of men in dark blue uniforms and set up in two rows. There was hardly a cry from the babies. Without proper care – without proper love – they were getting weaker. The men who'd carried them stood to attention behind the cots, waiting to be inspected by the woman now stepping out of the elevator door on the far side of the cavern. As Alison Beech marched towards them, Baldy on one side, Muscles on the other, and what seemed like an entire troop of white-coated scientists following behind, Eddie felt the hairs on the back of his head also stand to attention. They were going to find out what this was all about. And then, he suspected, they were going to die.

She stepped carefully in her high heels over what

looked like railway tracks – which Eddie presumed had once been used for mining coal or something from the mountain, but which now ended in a dead end against the far wall – as if she was on a modelling assignment for an expensive magazine. She flicked her hair back and pouted seductively. Eddie glanced at Mo. She was standing stiffly, with her hands bunched into fists. She was a tough wee thing, but she wasn't going to be able to punch her way out of this. As for Scuttles, sweating profusely, his left leg shaking involuntarily, he looked like he needed a trunk-load of headache tablets and a good lie-down.

Alison Beech didn't even look at them as she passed. She only had eyes for the babies. She clasped and unclasped her hands as she examined each one, her face a picture of delight, but her eyes – well, they were dark and hungry, and very, very frightening.

'Are they all well?' she purred.

'Yes ma'am,' said one of the scientists, who'd been preceding her to each cot, rapidly checking their temperatures by placing a plastic strip thermometer across their brows, pressing it down hard and then ripping it off as soon as he got the faintest reading.

'Isn't that a bonus?' said Alison Beech. 'I thought we'd lose at least a couple of the little piggies in transit.'

'Our formula only requires eight. So we could have lost four of them and we'd still be fine.'

'Well then, what shall we do? Send four of them back to their parents? Or just throw them in the mix as well?'

'Throw them in, ma'am. Be like adding extra beef to a fine stew.'

Eddie felt sick. Sick and angry. They were talking about the babies as if . . . well, exactly the way they were talking about them. Like they were ingredients in a stew. And he was standing there, doing nothing. NOTHING.

And that wasn't what he was best at. He was best at getting involved in things, and messing them up. That had been the story of his life in the city. Whatever he turned his hand to ended in disaster. But at least he had tried. Now he was standing idly by while this mad woman salivated over these helpless babies, standing like he was scared of his own shadow. He had to do something. It didn't matter if he messed it up this time. Whatever he did or said, if it ended in his own death or the death of Mo or Scuttles or the babies, it didn't matter, because they were clearly all going to die anyway.

'Hey you!' Eddie shouted. Everyone but Alison Beech turned towards him. The nearest guard thumped him in the back, but he hardly felt it. He was in the grip of his bad temper. 'I'm talking to you, you big long drink of water!'

Slowly, Alison Beech turned towards him.

'Are you talking to me, boy?'

'Of course I am, you manky old ironing board.'

Half a smile was chased across her face by a frown.

'What *are* you talking about?'

'I'm talking about you, you bloody big stick insect! Look at you, I can't believe people say you're beautiful! You look like something that's been pulled through a cheese grater. You look like—'

And then he was slapped hard across the face by Baldy and he went tumbling backwards.

He was back on his feet in a second, rushing forwards, determined to make some lasting impression on her, like a black eye or a fractured skull. But Baldy caught hold of his jacket and yanked him backwards, then, before he could regain his balance, he thrust him into the arms of two of the guards. He still wasn't finished and struggled hard against them, cursing and shouting at Alison Beech, but they held him firm.

Alison Beech came up to take a closer look at him. 'Oh yes – I remember you. Eddie, isn't it? Didn't I kill your mother?' And then she looked at her watch. 'Oh no – that's in about ten minutes.' She snorted with laughter. Eddie tried to swing for her, but again he was held firmly in check. 'Dear, dear, I understand you being upset. She seemed such a nice woman. Though rather plain. My condolences, in advance. If it makes you feel any better, it will be very quick, although rather painful. As these little piggies are about to find out. Quite unavoidable, I'm afraid.'

She turned back towards the babies.

'You're bloody mad!' Eddie screamed after her.

She stopped. Nobody had dared to call her mad before. Nobody had dared because she paid them huge amounts of money to work for her. And also because they were completely and utterly frightened of her. She turned back. Even in the midst of his anger Eddie noted that her eyes were narrower now, even more frightening.

'Mad? You think someone who's mad could build an empire like mine? You think someone who's mad could become the richest woman in the world? Do you think a madwoman could create a headquarters like *this*?'

'Yes,' said Eddie. 'You could do all of that and still be barking. And you are. Woof woof.'

She almost, almost snapped a hand out to slap him, but just managed to retain her composure. She even gave him the benefit of a cruel little smile. She cupped his chin in her hand and forced his head up. 'You're really quite brave for such a . . .' but she stopped when she realised that Eddie wasn't looking into her eyes as she'd intended, but down at her wrist and lower arm which were just visible where her sleeve had ridden up as she reached out for him. The skin around her wrist was very loose, and covered in dark, dark spots, like a rotting banana skin. She quickly dropped her hand from his chin and pulled the sleeve down. But Eddie had seen something, something he didn't yet understand, something which prompted a fresh burst of fury from Alison Beech. She wheeled away and yelled: 'Bring it out! Bring out the Crusher!'

Thirty-Five

The rumbling, which had seemed merely loud at first, became almost deafening as the wall at the back of the cave swung open and a machine, a contraption, an invention, an unholy terror, the like of which Eddie could never have imagined, began to slowly move towards them along what he had thought were disused mining tracks.

Eddie was born of an age when it was considered important that any new invention appeared slick, and modern, and cool; it could have no sharp edges, it could not fume or boil or roar; it had to be what we call user-friendly. Even if it was created to kill people, it still had to look pretty groovy. But this monstrosity was entirely different; it was the size of a slum dwelling and as loud as a jet exploding. Its massive bulk was encased in miles of black metal pipes which steamed and hissed and dripped as they fed a huge engine which in turn bled its power into two gigantic steel plates which were set opposite each other, like two sides in a war ready to commence battle.

Mo looked at Eddie as the infernal engine inched its way across the cavern floor. 'What is it?' she shouted above the din. And then repeated it, even louder.

'She called it the Crusher!' Eddie yelled back. 'I think that might be a clue!'

'But what's she going to . . . ?' Mo started to shout back, ignoring his sarcasm, but she stopped, because, really, she already knew.

Alison Beech hadn't built such a machine to crush grapes.

She hadn't spent years inventing the Crusher to perfect the art of the toasted sandwich.

Mo knew, Eddie knew and Scuttles knew that Alison Beech had ordered the creation of the machine for one reason and one reason alone.

Or twelve reasons.

Twelve little crying reasons whose terror couldn't be heard above the roar of the monster that would consume them. That would crush them.

'Why . . . ?!' Eddie screamed, but nobody could hear him either. Most certainly Alison Beech couldn't, standing imperiously, head held high, beaming with pride as the scientists guided the Crusher across the floor of the cavern to a pre-arranged position, then cut the engine. Even with the power switched off, it took several minutes of wheezing and panting for the engine to fall silent. As it gave its final hiss the air was filled with the cries of the babies, shaken and stirred in their cots by the approach of their doom, but they were ignored as the scientists surged forward, climbing up and then scrambling all over the machine, checking, checking, checking.

Eddie tried to shout at Alison Beech again, but he had shouted so much only a dry rasp emerged. It fell to Scuttles, dropping to his knees, shaking his head in horror, to voice all of their thoughts. 'My God,' he cried, 'what are you doing?'

Beech turned towards him, and said incredulously, 'Doing? What do you *think* I'm doing? I'm going to crush my babies!'

'But why?!'

'Why? Because I *can*!' She laughed. She gazed down the twin rows of cots. 'Because they're mine.'

'Just . . . for badness?' Scuttles asked, his voice barely more than a defeated whisper.

Alison Beech turned towards him. 'Badness? Of course not! It's the very opposite. Goodness, man, *goodness*. I have devoted my whole life to the science of goodness, of beauty, of health. And these little babies, they will advance that science. They are helping me, to help you. See, everyone benefits!'

When she saw both Eddie and Mo staring at her in horror she looked genuinely hurt and hurried up to them. 'Is that what you think, that I would hurt those little babies if there wasn't a really good reason for it?'

With her being so close, and the madness clear as Arctic air in her eyes, neither of them dared respond.

They didn't need to, because she was now gripped with the urgency of a born-again teacher with only days to live, determined to communicate as much as possible in the little time she had left. She turned and swept her hand over the outline of the Crusher. 'This,' she said with a flourish, 'this is what makes it all worthwhile! Twenty years ago I set my scientists a task, to invent a cream that would make me young again, that would take years off me. I didn't mean something that would make me *look* younger, something that would spirit away a few wrinkles – I wanted something that would actually *change* me. Make my skin exactly the same as a baby's, make my heart as fresh as a child's, repair my liver, replace my blood, let me start over. They worked and they worked and they worked, they tried everything, they killed a million mice in their experiments, they extracted DNA from children, from little babies in the womb, they grew little people in test tubes to harvest their blood, but nothing worked. They harnessed the most powerful computers in the world, they analysed every substance known to man, until finally, finally they came up with a formula. The only problem was that the most crucial element of that formula was – well, essence of baby. Not dead baby, not seriously ill baby, but live, healthy baby. They found that if they could capture the DNA in the very fraction of a second between life and death, between the final signal being sent from the brain and it being received by the body, then they could capture that very spark of life. And applying that to an adult, why, they could reverse the very ageing process! Of course it's all been theory until today – but now I have my babies and as soon as the machine is ready, then I'll have my magic cream! Oh, don't look so shocked, children, they're only little puppies, they don't know anything yet, and besides, they won't feel a thing, apart from a very brief moment of excruciating pain.'

She turned to inspect the machine again.

'But please, Mrs Beech . . .' It was Mo.

Alison Beech turned, slightly irritated and snapped, 'It's *Miss*.'

'Miss – I'm sorry. But ... you're so young and beautiful, why would you even need such a cream?'

Eddie thought Mo was being quite naïve if she was seeking to win over Alison Beech with compliments, but stranger things happen in the world, especially when you're dealing with someone who's clearly bonkers. Alison Beech's manner changed instantly, she stroked her long blonde hair for several moments and smiled fondly at Mo. 'Tell me, child, how old do you think I am?'

Mo glanced at Eddie for help.

Eddie was young, but old enough to know not to mess with a woman's age. He quickly ran the figures over in his head – Alison Beech had to be older than she looked, because she surely couldn't have built up such a huge business in just a few years. His dad had once advised him, if a woman asks you to guess her age, decide what age she is in your head, then take ten years off it. Eddie mouthed at Mo: 'Twenty-five.'

'Twenty ... three?' Mo said hesitantly.

Alison Beech clapped her hands together. 'How sweet!' Then snapped angrily, 'Try again!'

'Twenty . . . four . . . ?'

'Again!'

'Twenty-six?'

Alison Beech suddenly grabbed Mo by her shirt and pulled her close. 'Close, my dear, close enough to deserve a kiss.' She puckered up her wondrously thick and seductive red lips, Mo cowered back. 'What's wrong, my dear, don't you like my lovely lips? Wouldn't you like lips like these? Well?' Mo managed to give the slightest nod. 'Good. Then have them!' And with a dramatic swipe of her hand, Alison Beech ripped her own lips off.

Really.

Of course, they weren't real. They were false lips. Her actual lips were as thin as starving worms and as cracked as an old pavement.

Alison Beech cackled. 'What about my hair, do you like *that*?'

Before Mo could respond Alison Beech had dragged off her hair – a wig – leaving a pock-marked scalp dotted with pockets of jagged grey fluff.

'What about my teeth? Aren't they perfect?'

And she pulled out her false teeth. She cupped them in her hand and began to move towards Mo making a biting motion with them, top set cracking against bottom set.

Mo backed away, but the guards stopped her from going any further – although they didn't look too comfortable with this new vision of Alison Beech either.

But she wasn't finished. She removed a false nose, false ears with built-in hearing aids; she stripped away eye-lashes, contact lenses, a layer of plastic skin from her face and hands and feet and legs and arms until there was a pile of fake body parts lying scattered on the ground around her.

'Do you still think I'm beautiful?!' Alison Beech screamed. 'I'm seventy-eight years old! In an industry that demands beauty and perfection! I cannot keep up this charade for ever! I need to be young! *Do you understand, girl?* I *need* to be YOUNG!'

Mo said something so quietly that Eddie couldn't quite catch it.

Neither apparently could Alison Beech. She leaned in with her ancient ears and hissed: 'What was that?'

Mo held her eyes for several long moments, then repeated it.

'You'll never be young again.'

Fury boiled in Alison Beech's eyes. She slapped Mo hard, knocking her back into the arms of the guards. Eddie strained forward in a vain attempt to protect her, but again was held in place. Scuttles just watched blankly.

Alison Beech turned abruptly and snapped: 'Turn on the Crusher! Let's see if it actually works!' She pointed back at Mo. 'Take this little girl and squash her!'

Thirty-Six

Forty miles away in the Royal Victoria Hospital, a doctor who had once taken an oath promising to devote his life to the practice of medicine, a doctor who had studied hard, who had performed many difficult operations, who had earned the gratitude of literally thousands of people for his wonderful work and caring manner, was about to kill Eddie's mother.

He was not happy about it, but he would do it nevertheless.

Alison Beech had personally pleaded with him to do it. Mrs Malone, the poor patient, was suffering from an incurable disease of the brain. It had already reduced her to a quivering wreck requiring her confinement in the hospital's mental wing, but it would very quickly develop into a huge tumour which would cause her to suffer a long, slow and agonising death. Mrs Malone was an old family friend, and Alison Beech could not bear to see her suffer. Of course Dr Alastair Holmes wasn't about to administer a lethal dose of drugs merely because someone – even someone as important as Alison Beech – asked him to. He was about to do it because he had studied Mrs Malone's medical report and knew what a horrific death she was facing. He felt dreadfully, dreadfully sorry for her. Dr Holmes had no reason to suspect that the report had been faked, as it had, or that his superiors, the men who ran the hospital, had co-operated in the faking of it because Alison Beech had threatened to cut off funding for the new wing and indeed withdraw all of her financial support, thus possibly causing hundreds of deaths, not to mention setting back research by many years and causing misery and unemployment throughout the community. They decided it was the lesser of two evils to co-operate with her. There was also the fact that she paid them personally a huge amount of money. Bribery and corruption. That was how Alison Beech worked.

It wasn't as if the poor woman would die right there in front of him. No, there was a chemical compound they used occasionally which when injected caused the patient to fall into a deep sleep and then just drift towards death over the course of several days. Dr Holmes sighed, loaded the syringe, packed it in a small case, checked the security code for the mental wing, then headed for the elevator.

Eddie's mum was always one for making the best of a bad situation. Her husband had left her, and she had reacted by moving to a new city, a new job and a new life. She had met a nice man in Bernard Scuttles. Now that nice man was suspected of being involved in the dreadful theft of twelve babies, her son was missing, and she was being held captive in the mental wing of her own hospital. She did not yet know that Alison Beech was responsible for this, only that the two men who had broken into her apartment and kidnapped her – one of them bald, one of them very muscular – had demanded to know the whereabouts of the babies, which she obviously couldn't tell them – and then after receiving a phone call had abruptly changed their attitude and dumped her here in what they had described as 'the loony bin'.

Now, a lot of people would have been frightened by the patients in the mental wing. Some were locked up there because they were extremely violent, some because they talked to strange invisible people, some because they spent their whole days banging their heads against walls and had to wear crash helmets, some because they couldn't eat stew without pouring it into their pockets, some couldn't speak and some couldn't stop speaking. Some nurses didn't want anything to do with them, some treated them cruelly, but Mrs Malone, even though she'd only been at the hospital a few weeks, had all the time in the world for them. It wasn't their fault they weren't well. Their biggest problem, she often thought, was that nobody loved them.

So, when she was thrown into the mental wing and the door locked behind her, she wasn't afraid, and her fellow patients weren't afraid of her. It was a dirty, stinking, badly-lit place; the food was appalling and shoved through slots in the door rather than served; the toilets hadn't been cleaned in weeks; the other nurses barely visited, but when they did they were escorted by burly men with cattle prods who gave any trouble-makers a swift electric shock. But there was barely any trouble, because so many of the patients were kept on such a heavy regime of drugs that they were hardly able to function. Eddie's mum was supposed to take the drugs as well, but she'd been a nurse for long enough to know all the tricky places to hide pills. As far as they were concerned she *was* drugged, but she was watching, watching all the time, although it seemed to her that there was no prospect of escape. The doors were controlled by a security code she did not know, and the nurses were convinced that she had a brain disease and so blamed that for her wild stories about kidnapping.

While she waited for something to happen, or for some opportunity to escape, she busied herself with the welfare of the patients. She was kind to them, and they in turn were kind to her. The woman with the crash helmet stopped banging her head against the wall and made her a cup of cold tea. (They weren't allowed boiling water in case they burned themselves.) The woman with stew in her pockets got her a biscuit, and the man who talked to his invisible friends introduced them all to her. They turned out to be interesting company, even though they didn't exist. Eddie's mum was still deeply worried about her son, about Scuttles, about the babies, but she wasn't worried about herself.

Like her son, she thought that everything would turn out okay in the end.

She wasn't aware that she was less than three minutes away from a lethal injection.

She wasn't aware that Dr Holmes was at that

very moment standing by the doors to the mental wing, with a security guard armed with a cattle prod on either side of him.

Dr Holmes keyed in the security code, then pulled at the door.

But it didn't open.

He keyed it in again, in case he'd somehow pressed the wrong number, but still it wouldn't budge. He checked the codes with the security guards, and yes, indeed, they did have the right one. So why wasn't it opening? If the guards had bothered to check their security cameras, say about half an hour previously, they might have noted a small boy loitering by the entrance to the mental wing. They might have observed him hurry across and pour some sort of liquid into the locking mechanism and then scamper away. They might have recognised a Reservoir Pup.

Eddie's mum was blissfully unaware of all this drama until sparks became visible through a small hole in the door to the mental wing.

Somebody was using a blowtorch.

Still, it was nothing to be concerned about. So somebody had messed up the codes. It happened. She returned to combing the long hair of one of the female patients, who was almost purring with gratitude.

But she was then disturbed by another sound, a loud knocking which was coming from the window behind her.

She glanced back and saw the woman with the crash helmet standing by the glass. Eddie's mum asked her nicely to stop making such a racket.

'It's not me, Mrs,' said the crash-helmeted lady, 'it's the kid outside.'

Eddie's mum laughed and thought to herself, *Yeah, right, we're on the seventeenth floor.*

Then the knocking came again. And it wasn't the woman, for she'd now stepped away from the window. Eddie's mum clutched her chest in shock, for she could now see that there was indeed a child visible through the barred window – and it appeared to be floating in mid-air.

Thirty-Seven

The Crusher roared back to life.

It may have looked ancient and decrepit, it may have belched steam and spat boiling water, but it was designed to perfection. One switch and it was ready to go, ready to crush, ready to destroy, ready to squish the Andytown Albino. The guards frog-marched Mo forward. Eddie tried to spring after her and managed to wriggle out of his guard's grasp, just for a second, before he was struck hard from behind and tumbled over and then they were upon him, pinning him to the ground.

'You can't!' Eddie screamed, straining against them. 'You can't do this!'

'Ah, but I can,' said Alison Beech. 'It's called getting rid of the witnesses, we'll squash her down to a liquid, and then we can all have a little drink of her. How about that?'

'You're mad!'

'Sticks and stones . . .'

'And you're ugly!'

'Will break my bones . . .'

'You were never beautiful!'

'But names will never hurt me. Although frankly I can't be bothered with nursery rhymes, so boring, don't you think?' She thought for a moment. 'Tell you what. Bring him as well, we'll squish two for the price of one.'

Eddie stopped struggling. 'You're not *that* ugly,' he said, but it was too late, he was hauled to his feet and dragged up the steps to stand beside Mo.

'That wasn't very smart,' she said.

Eddie shrugged helplessly.

In front of them the two huge metal plates had begun to move against each other, gaining speed all the time, and were soon cracking against each other so quickly that they became virtually indistinguishable.

Eddie put his hand out to Mo, and she took it.

'Sorry about this,' he said.

'Too bloody late now,' she snapped back. But she followed it with a little smile. She squeezed his hand. 'When we get out of this, Eddie, we should form our own gang. Nobody will be able to stop us.'

Eddie caught himself nodding, then shook himself back to reality. 'What do you mean, *when* we get out of this? We're about to be squashed, you numbskull.'

She took a deep breath. 'You're such a pessimist, Eddie.'

Then she closed her eyes, and waited for the push. Eddie closed his as well.

This was it, the end of his life.

There was a sudden commotion behind them and Eddie's eyes snapped open again. Scuttles had struggled free of his guards and was now rushing towards Alison Beech. It was a hopeless attempt to attack her, for his way was quickly blocked. As four of the guards held him back he shouted: 'They're only kids! Let them go! Take me instead!'

Alison Beech looked impressed. 'You'd sacrifice yourself for these little animals?'

'Yes!'

'Well. You do surprise me. I *was* going to let you go – you would have been thrown in prison for stealing the babies, but at least you'd have been alive. But I'll tell you what – yes, I'll squash you, but no, I won't spare the children, because you can never trust a child. I'll flatten you all! All for one, and one for all, isn't that what they say?!' Alison Beech clapped her hands together. 'All right, enough talk, let's get it over with and then on with the main business of the day!'

Scuttles was bundled up the steps to stand beside Eddie and Mo.

'That wasn't very clever,' said Eddie.

'He's not joining our gang,' said Mo. 'He's not smart enough.'

Scuttles didn't get that, here, at the very end of their lives, they were only joking. He probably didn't even hear them. He couldn't take his eyes from the plates, moving so fast that they were a just a blur.

Muscles was standing behind them now.

He would push them one by one. Or he would push them all together.

It didn't really matter.

'Five!' Baldy shouted.

'Four!' yelled Muscles.

Eddie thought about his mum and his dad, and how much he loved them.

'Three!' shouted Baldy.

Eddie wondered if there was a God. He hoped there was, because he was praying desperately to Him. Or Her. He wanted his very last thought to be something good and worthy and important, but instead he found that he was thinking about whether he would come back in his next life as a hedgehog.

'Two!'

'One!'

THE END.

Or so it seemed.

The last thing Eddie heard was a loud bang. Then there was a scream. Then he experienced a kind of floating sensation. If this is death, he thought, then it's really not too bad, it feels like I'm flying to another world.

And then he opened his eyes and realised that he actually *was* flying – not to another world, but through the air.

Then they all landed in a heap on the hard rock floor of the cavern while pandemonium broke out all around them.

Smoke was billowing out of the Crusher, shards of metal were shooting high into the air, half a dozen pipes had split from the body of the machine and were twisting this way and that like electric eels, spraying their boiling fluids everywhere. Eddie could hear Alison Beech yelling at the scientists through the smoke, and the scientists yelling at each other. He caught glimpses of the guards rushing about with fire extinguishers trying to put out the fire. Eddie, Mo and Scuttles remained on the ground, rubbing their bruised limbs, thanking God that the explosion had hurled all three of them backwards rather than forwards into the jaws of the machine.

Despite the best efforts of Beech's men, the smoke was getting thicker and thicker. Eddie had no idea what had gone wrong with the machine, and he didn't care – all he knew was that they were alive, and for the moment they were being ignored. They might never have another opportunity to esc—

And then he was grabbed from behind, and a hood was pulled down over his head. What had been merely hazy and indistinct because of the smoke suddenly became completely black. He was pulled to his feet and pushed and prodded away across the floor of the cavern.

Thirty-Eight

Eddie's mum peered through the glass and bars at the boy beyond. Now that she was much closer she could see that he wasn't floating, or even flying – he was hanging. He was connected to some kind of harness, and that was joined to a rope that disappeared somewhere above him.

She cupped her hands and shouted: 'What do you want?'

At exactly the same time the boy yelled: 'Stay back!'

This had the effect of neither of them hearing each other. She was about to shout again, but then jumped back in surprise at a sudden eruption of sparks outside. 'Oh my word,' she said, clutching her chest.

The boy, who couldn't have been more than ten or eleven, had pulled a mask down over his face. He was using a blowtorch to remove the bars from the window. She glanced back at the door to the mental wing. A definite hole had appeared in the door above the lock mechanism.

What on earth was going on?

It was like some kind of mad race.

When she looked back to the window she was surprised to see that a second boy was now hanging in the air. He was also operating a blowtorch. She didn't know it, but his name was Bacon.

All of the patients in the mental wing – at least those who could walk, and those who weren't talking to invisible people – had now gathered to watch this competition. Some stood by the door, others by the window; some rushed between the two, giving excited commentary the whole way. They clapped their hands and jumped with excitement. Somebody was placing bets with *Monopoly* money.

Eddie's mum heard a wrenching sound, and saw that not one but two of the four window bars were now missing. Back at the door the hole had encircled almost three quarters of the lock. Another few minutes and they'd be able to push the broken lock in and open the door.

Behind her a third bar gave way. Just one to go – with both blowtorches now concentrating on it.

What was she going to do?

Maybe the people at the door were here to rescue

her. Maybe they were here just to open a stuck door. Or maybe they were the very ones who'd put her here in the first place and were now planning something much worse!

But what of the boys at the window? What did *they* have to do with it? They looked like some of the street urchins who caused havoc around the hospital. And what could they possibly do once they succeeded in breaking in? Was there going to be a fight? She certainly couldn't risk any of the patients getting hurt.

The final bar gave way. Bacon, his fist encased in a protective glove, reached forward and punched the glass hard, shattering it instantly. At almost exactly that moment the circle was completed around the door lock and it was pushed through, landing with a crack on the linoleum floor to cheers from the patients grouped around it. A moment later the door swung open and Dr Holmes and three security guards stepped through the smoke into the mental wing. They were immediately surrounded by the excited patients. The security guards drew their cattle prods and began to force their way through while Dr Holmes scanned the wing for Mrs Malone.

'Missus!' Bacon hissed from the window. 'This

way!' He was reaching out his hand to her.

What was the boy talking about? If he was so brave, why wasn't he coming in? Eddie's mum shook her head. She looked back towards the door. The patients were now screaming as they fled from the cattle prods. *But surely they won't do that to me, I'm a nurse, they know I'm a . . .*

'Mrs Malone! Please! It's your only chance!'

She shook her head. 'Don't be ridiculous! I'm sure if I reason with these gentlemen they'll realise that there's been some colossal misunder—'

At that point they spotted her, and she spotted Dr Holmes lifting the syringe from its case.

She didn't like needles at the best of times, and this certainly wasn't the best of times.

Eddie's mum reached up to the window frame, took a firm grip of it, then pulled herself up until she was standing in the open window.

'Don't look down!' Bacon shouted.

Of course she looked down.

And nearly fell.

It was bloody miles to the ground.

The hard, concrete ground.

She felt dizzy, her legs almost wilted under her.

She would have dropped if Bacon hadn't put his shoulder against her body and held her in place.

Then the other boy reached around her and attached a third harness.

'Ready?' said Bacon.

'Ready for—?'

But before she could finish Bacon had withdrawn his support and she fell from the window. She opened her mouth to scream, but no sound would come out. She was terrified beyond sound. What little breath was left in her lungs was jolted from her as her fall was suddenly halted. She hung there for several moments, swinging helplessly in the wind, then Bacon screamed: 'Go! Go! Go!'

She was suddenly yanked upwards, the boys ascending on either side of her, taking an arm each for further support.

She passed the open window, then the next floor and the next; curious patients looked out at her. She looked back down and saw the doctor a   n   d the security guards gesturing up at her and they appeared to be shouting, but their words were lost on the breeze. She looked up and saw boys peering cautiously from the roof while others supervised three pulleys which had been secured to the edge.

'Come on! Come on!' one of them yelled.

Now that she was actually being propelled through the air, certain death below and uncertain adventure above, Eddie's mum found much to her surprise that she was actually enjoying it.

When they finally pulled her up over the edge, she had a smile on her face. 'Wooo-hoooo!' she exclaimed as the kids carefully guided her down on to the roof and removed her harness. Bacon and the other boy appeared beside her.

'That was fantast—' she began to say.

'Let's go!' Bacon shouted.

She was being ushered quickly across the roof towards a small door.

'Where are we . . . what are we . . .'

Alarms were now sounding throughout the hospital.

As they reached the door another kid appeared and thrust a doctor's white coat at her. She pulled it on as they descended a narrow set of stairs. At the bottom, which was just beyond the fire doors on the east side of the hospital's top floor, Bacon handed her a stethoscope and a pair of glasses. As she put both of them on a girl reached up and pulled her hair back into a ponytail. Bacon pointed down the corridor.

'This place will be crawling with security in a minute, just keep walking, try to look important, they'll ignore you.'

'I can't, they'll recognise—'

'No they won't. Believe me. It's all about confidence. Now, get moving.'

Eddie's mum took a step forward. 'But what about you?'

She looked at the kids. There were eight of them. Small in stature, big in heart.

'Don't worry about us, we know this place like the back of our hands. Once you're outside, go to the McDonalds on Great Victoria Street. Captain Black will meet you there. I expect you'll want to know about Eddie.'

'Eddie . . . is he . . . ?

But Bacon merely shook his head, gave her the thumbs-up, signalled for the others to follow him, then set off running down the corridor.

Eddie's mum watched them for a moment, took a deep breath, and started walking in the opposite direction.

Thirty-Nine

Eddie learned not to speak during the journey, because each time he started to say something he got a thump in the back. They walked for about thirty minutes, up tunnels and down them, clambering sightlessly over rocks and slipping uncontrollably down sudden inclines; several times he was pushed roughly to the ground and held there until some supposed threat had passed. In the far distance he heard dogs barking and people shouting. When they finally reached their destination he heard many voices, but they were all delivered in such a rushed whisper that they were rendered indistinct. He was guided on to the ground, but his hood was not removed. As far as he could judge he was lying on the floor of a small cave. He could smell fire and was vaguely aware of its heat, but it was a different smell to the acrid smoke given off by the burning Crusher, it was more like one of the coal fires his dad used to set in their old house in Groomsport.

There was movement around him in the cave,

soft padding footsteps, more whispers. Then they seemed to drift away and he took the chance of whispering: 'Mo?', while tensing up ready for a smack.

'Eddie?' She was close. Her voice was small and nervous. 'Where are we?'

'I don't know ...'

There was movement near them again, and he smelled food. His hood was pulled up only as far as his nose; one hand was guided to a bowl, the other had a spoon thrust into it.

'Eat,' said a rough voice.

Eddie had not eaten for as long as could remember, unless you counted the eggs. He had not been aware of being hungry, but suddenly he was ravenous. He spooned the food – a type of stew – hungrily into his mouth, spilling much of it, but not caring. And then he thought suddenly – stew, babies, babies in a stew – what if this was some twisted joke Alison Beech was playing on them? Feeding them the very creatures they had come to save.

He felt ill. He put the bowl down. He tried to stop himself from being sick again. He closed his eyes and tried to steady his breathing. Every bone in his body ached. He had been living in a state of terror for as long as he could remember. He was alive, but for how long? He had to rest, gather his strength. He wasn't dead yet. Still time to escape. Plan. But rest. Eyes closed. Tired. Just for a moment – sleep. No. Yes. Just a little shut-eye, two minutes, no more, two minutes . . .

Four hours later and his snores were really starting to annoy his captors. So they pulled his hood off and shook him and as he gradually came awake they stepped back. Eddie rubbed at his eyes. Where was he? Someone had . . . ? What about Mo . . . ? It was only when his eyes were drawn to the brightness of the fire that he realised he was no longer wearing the hood. And then as he grew more accustomed to the light he became aware of the figures standing in the shadows, watching him.

'I . . .' he began, then started again. 'Who are you? What do you . . . ?'

The closest figure bent forward into the light.

And Eddie went: 'Ah!' and shot back hard against the wall of the cave.

It was his eyes.

The left eye was fine.

So was the right eye.

It was the eye in the middle that scared the pants off Eddie.

'Do not be afraid,' said the three-eyed boy.

For that's what he was, just a boy, not much older than Eddie. Eddie shook himself. 'I'm not . . . really,' he said and forced himself to shuffle forwards again into the light. As he did he began to make out his other captors – perhaps a dozen of them watching him. None of the others had three eyes, thank goodness. But one of them had three arms, one had no arms, one was lacking a nose, another had webbed hands, there was a girl with no ears – they were all deformed in different ways.

'We are not any more deformed than you are,' said the boy with three eyes.

Eddie was stunned. 'You . . . know what I'm thinking?'

'We hear certain . . . thoughts, impressions of thoughts, really. And you look as odd to us as we must to you.' He turned to the others. 'Imagine – he only has two eyes.'

They all laughed. One of them barked. They were an odd group.

'I don't understand . . . who are you?'

'My name is Diet.'

'Diet?'

'Yes. Diet Coke.' He turned and waved around the

280

group. 'This is Snickers, Beans, Mild New Fairy . . .'

'Are you winding me up? Those are your nicknames, right?'

'No, these are our names.'

'Your parents named you after *groceries*?'

Diet Coke shook his head. 'We have no parents.'

The girl he had called Beans came up beside him and put a hand on his arm. 'Diet – that is not true. We have one parent.'

Diet Coke patted her arm. 'This is true. We share one parent.'

They all began to nod in agreement.

'Alison Beech,' said a familiar voice. It was Mo, coming through the mouth of the cave, smiling happily. 'Eddie – you've been asleep for hours. I went for a bit of an explore.'

Eddie was confused. 'They allowed you to . . .'

'Eddie – they're not our enemies, they're our friends. They saved us. They sabotaged the Crusher and rescued us.'

Eddie looked at Diet Coke. 'I don't understand. Why would you do that? What are you doing here? Why do you have such weird names? And how is Alison Beech your mother?'

Mo came up beside him and took his arm. 'Look at them, Eddie, can't you guess?'

He looked and he saw and suddenly he understood. 'Experiments,' he said.

Diet nodded. 'For many years, Alison Beech and her scientists have been trying to create life, perfect life. Many children have been born in her laboratories. Most do not survive, many are killed when they are shown to be . . . different . . . but some whose differences are not immediately apparent are allowed to live, at least until the extent of their difference can be judged. Over the years a few of us have managed to escape into the tunnels and live off the waste left by all of her hundreds of scientists. From time to time we raid the laboratories and rescue whoever we can. I myself was rescued when I was only two weeks old.'

Eddie didn't know what to say. He managed a weak 'I'm sorry.'

Diet shook his head. 'Don't be. We are happy.'

'You live in these caves all the time?'

'Most of the time. Sometimes we go out into the forest at night. We steal from the farms when we can't get enough fresh food.'

'But don't you want to go out into the real world?'

'This *is* the real world, Eddie,' said Beans. 'Besides, look at Diet Coke. How would he survive out there? Can you imagine him trying to buy a pair of glasses?'

Diet Coke blinked his three eyes angrily at her for several moments, then abruptly burst into laughter. He put his arm around her and kissed her on the top of the head.

Mo smiled at Eddie. 'Isn't it incredible?'

Eddie nodded. Though he immediately liked Diet Coke and the rest of them, he couldn't help but wonder why they had rescued them.

'Because we will do anything that will disrupt the evil work of Alison Beech,' said Mild New Fairy. Eddie swallowed. They'd read his thoughts again.

Diet Coke knelt down beside him. His three eyes were blue and intense. 'She has grown more desperate of late. Bad enough creating life and then destroying it, but now she has realised that she is never going to make the perfect child. We have watched her build that machine for five years but we were never sure what it was for until the babies arrived. We have only caused it minor damage. It will be ready again in a few hours, and this time it will be guarded properly. But we cannot allow her to kill them. We were created in a test tube, without love. But those babies were created by men and women with love. We can be sacrificed and nobody will care. They cannot.' He stood up and addressed the entire group. 'We must prepare for war!'

Forty

They called themselves the Forgotten, and they scurried along the tunnels at a tremendous speed, their eyes well used to the dark. Eddie banged his head, his knees, his shoulders, as he tried to keep pace with them. He wished to God he still had the night vision glasses. Mo fared even worse, her weak albino eyesight rendering her virtually blind in the blackness of the mining tunnels. Diet Coke would only allow them to use the weakest of torches, a slither of rag dipped in oil and set alight, which only illuminated a few feet at a time. It was virtually useless for travelling quickly. They took a different, more difficult route back towards the cavern, and twice had to extinguish the light as the barking of guard dogs echoed along the long disused passages. All told there were twenty-three of them, ranging from a four year old who scurried ahead of the main group scouting for trouble, to Diet Coke, who at sixteen was the eldest.

Eddie wondered what had happened to the Forgotten who had rescued Diet Coke.

'They died,' Diet Coke said, having heard his thought.

'Oh – sorry,' said Eddie, aware that it sounded painfully inadequate. Then he banged his knee on an outcrop of rock, which took his mind off it. He let out a yelp. Mo asked him if he was okay, then hurried him on. The Forgotten were not for waiting.

Eddie was ashamed to say that the fate of Bernard J. Scuttles had not even crossed his mind until Mo asked Diet Coke about him. It appeared that they could have rescued him as well, but decided not to. They simply didn't trust him. Not because they knew anything about his background, which from Eddie's point of view would have been reason enough, but because he was a man, and the only men they had encountered in their short lives had tried to hunt them down and kill them in the labyrinth of tunnels that made up their world.

As they ran they began to hear a familiar roaring sound, which grew in intensity as they approached the mouth of a narrow tunnel. The Crusher. Diet Coke signalled for them to stop, and for Eddie and Mo to extinguish their torches. They then edged forward and peered down to the floor of the cavern. The Crusher lay several hundred metres away, puffing and spitting as before. Although there were still several scientists examining its main engine it was clearly back to something close to working order. Eddie scanned the area around it, but there was no sign of the babies' cots.

Diet Coke, Eddie and Mo crept back into the tunnel, then knelt with the others in a circle. Diet Coke went over the plan for the final time: they would split into three groups; the first, largest group would mount an assault on the Crusher; this wasn't meant to destroy the machine, but to draw the guards into pursuing the group back into the tunnels. A second group would make its way up to ground level and either distract or overpower the guards there. The third group, made up of Eddie and Mo, would take advantage of both attacks by the Forgotten to rescue the babies from a small cave at the back of the cavern. If the guards there had not been drawn away, they would have to find some means of getting rid of them. They would then have to carry all twelve babies to one of the lorries parked nearby and make their escape.

Eddie could imagine about a hundred and twenty things that could go wrong with the plan.

And, with his luck, most of them would.

* * *

One of the guards had put food out for the dogs. Muscles was busy taking it away from them – he thought hungry dogs made better hunters, and they still had kids to catch and kill – when something struck him hard on the arm. He turned, thinking for a moment that one of the scientists might have dropped a spanner off the top of the Crusher, but no, there was a rock on the ground beside him. It would have broken the arm of a lesser man. He looked up towards the roof of the cavern. Occasionally rocks did dislodge themselves. But when a loud, echoing cry went up, and dozens of rocks began to rain down all around, he realised they were under attack.

The scientists were shouting and scrambling off the Crusher as the rocks clanged off the vibrating metal. They knocked out guards, they struck the dogs and made them howl, they smashed into the chairs that had been set out for Alison Beech and the chief scientists to watch the crushing of the babies and the extraction of their vital fluids.

Muscles ducked down under the Crusher for cover. The cry came again – it was like a shriek a ghost might make, and it set the hairs on the back of his neck erect. He peered cautiously out from

288

the shelter of the machine and saw a light flickering away in the darkness, far across the floor of the cavern. There was someone standing there with a burning torch in his hand. Someone . . . or some*thing*, because it appeared to have three arms. It held a torch in one hand, and a rock in each of two others.

He . . . it . . . stamped a foot into the thick dust of the cavern floor and shouted: 'This is for the father I will never have!'

Then it threw the rocks in rapid succession.

Two cracked off the Crusher, another knocked one of the dogs unconscious.

Then there was another torch, about a dozen yards from the first, and this time the creature had three legs and four arms.

'This is for the mother who will never love me!' it yelled.

And it too heaved rocks at the Crusher.

Then another torch, and another, and another, until there were fifteen spread across the floor of the cavern like lighthouses in a dark sea. Each of the creatures had some kind of deformity.

Where one had let out a cry before, now they all cried together, a terrible wail which echoed off the walls.

'This is for the children who will never be!' they all shouted together.

And then rocks rained down with a much more terrifying intensity, cracking into the Crusher, bursting pipes, cracking the engine, knocking the scientists still clinging to it to the ground far below.

At this point Alison Beech, roused by the sounds of the attack, appeared at the mouth of the tunnel behind the Crusher. She screamed when she saw the damage that was being done to it, then screamed again as she followed the trajectory of the falling rocks back across the floor to the torches and the Forgotten.

'Destroy those animals! Shoot them!'

Muscles, Baldy and the other guards needed no further encouragement. They had had enough of cowering down. Alison Beech rarely let them use their guns, preferring to smooth her way with bribery and threats, but now she was taking them off the leash, just as they were now releasing their dogs. Baldy drew his revolver and waved the guards forwards. The attacking force was either tiring or running out of ammunition, because the number of rocks falling was now much reduced. Baldy began to run. 'Get them!' he screamed. 'Fire at will!'

The guards began to shoot.

But just as they did the torches began to go out. First from the left, then from the right, one by one they were being extinguished, plunging the floor of the cavern into murky darkness. Finally there was only one left in the centre. They had never seen Diet Coke before, they didn't know his name, but he stood there defiantly as the approaching guards concentrated their gunfire on the only point of light on that side of the Cavern.

Diet Coke raised a fist and shouted: 'We are the Forgotten, but you will never forget us!'

And then he stepped back into the darkness, leaving only the burning torch. When Baldy reached it seconds later there was no sign of the weird three-eyed creature, nor indeed of any of the others. They had disappeared. Beams from proper electric torches now swamped the area. The guards' attack on the Forgotten had been somewhat disorganised, but now, with more of them arriving, with their dogs barking furiously, Baldy was quickly able to organise them into squads and oversee a proper pursuit of the creatures through the tunnels. He would find them, he was sure of that, and when he did he would kill them all.

* * *

Eddie and Mo had watched the beginning of the attack crouched down low to the south of the Crusher. They had never seen anything like it in their lives. They had known the Forgotten for only a few hours, but could never have guessed that they would show such bravery, such violence.

Baldy was just leading the first charge against them when Mo pulled at Eddie's arm and whispered, 'Come on, we haven't time.'

Eddie nodded and followed. There were lights in this part of the cavern roof, but they were partially blocked by the huge bulk of the Crusher, so they were able to travel quickly in a kind of semi-darkness. They circled behind the chairs laid out for Alison Beech. They could just about hear her conferring with her scientists. Even with the intensity of the attack on the Crusher, it seemed that the damage had been largely superficial. There would only be a short delay.

They hurried on until they could see the mouth of the small cave where the babies were being kept. They couldn't see them, because beyond the entrance the cave sloped down and round, but they could hear them. There were two guards pacing anxiously, gazing towards the sounds of distant battle.

'What were they?' one of them was saying.

'I don't bloody know, kids dressed up.'

'Bloody weren't, bloody more like leprechauns or something.'

'Yeah, right, leprechauns – like *they* exist.'

'Either way, how come they get to do all the shooting?' He took out his gun. 'I want to shoot me one of them, whatever the hell they are.'

The other guard took out his gun as well. 'They're havin' all the fun, why can't we shoot something?'

'I didn't sign up to stand in a bloody cave all night. I signed up to shoot things.'

'Me too.'

'They're only babies, they ain't goin' anywhere.'

'Dead right there, mate.'

'C'mon – let's go, no-one'll ever know. I'm gonna shoot me a leprechaun.'

'They aren't bloody leprechauns!'

Whatever they were, both guards were determined to kill them. They hurried away to join the battle.

It was a stroke of luck.

Eddie and Mo darted into the mouth of the cave, then cautiously began to descend. They turned one corner, then another, and saw a light glowing from around a third.

'What if there's another guard?' Eddie hissed.

'Then we attack,' said Mo.

Eddie nodded, as if it was the most natural thing in the world.

They approached the third corner, the cries of the babies growing louder all the time. They were much too young to understand what danger they were in, but they were certainly aware that something wasn't right. No loving parents, no regular feeding, damp and dirty for long stretches, huge bangs, constant travelling; the only good things in their lives were the familiar, calming words now being sung to them by Bernard J. Scuttles.

He had lifted up one of the most upset babies, and was focussing the soft words of the song on it, when there was sudden movement around the bend. He was hugging the baby to him, determined to protect it at all costs, when Eddie and Mo stepped into the light.

'I thought you were . . .' he stammered. He tried to move towards them, but was held in place by the same chain and strap combination that Baldy had restrained him with back in the warehouse.

'We thought you were too,' said Eddie. 'But no such luck.'

Mo quickly examined the two rows of cots, then shook her head at Eddie. 'There's too many of them, we'll never get them all out in time.'

Eddie nodded. 'Then we'll put them all in one.'

'It's too many, Eddie, they'll get squashed.'

'Not as badly as they will out there.' He thumbed back towards the Crusher. 'Okay, Mo, go get the wheels.'

Mo nodded, then hurried back up the tunnel.

Eddie took the first baby out of Scuttles' arms, and placed it in the sturdiest looking of the cots with one of the other babies. He then turned to lift the next baby. Scuttles rattled his chain. 'Get me out of this, Eddie, I'll help.'

Eddie ignored him.

'Eddie, please.'

'What about my mum?'

'This isn't the time!'

'It's *exactly* the time.'

'Okay! All right! I've already promised to leave her alone!'

'I want you to resign from your job and move to another country.'

'You think I'll even *have* a job after this? Okay – okay, yes, I'll do it, I'll resign, now just get these bloody things off of me!'

Eddie now had seven babies in the one cot. Mo was right, there wasn't much room. He lifted the eight and the ninth together and squeezed them in.

As he gathered the tenth and eleventh he said, 'The problem is, Bernie, I just don't think I can trust you.'

'Yes, you can!'

He put numbers ten and eleven on top of the other babies, creating a second layer. It wasn't exactly straight out of a child care manual, but he had no alternative.

He gathered up number twelve just as Mo came running back down the tunnel.

'Piece of cake!' she exclaimed, and jangled a set of keys at Eddie.

Eddie nodded, then lowered the final baby into the cot.

'Eddie!'

Mo glanced at Scuttles. 'What's his problem?'

'He wants to come with us.'

'What do you expect!'

'I expect him to keep his word!'

'I will!' Scuttles shouted, 'Now for God's sake, let me go!'

Eddie finally nodded.

But it then took longer than they could really afford to locate a rock large enough to break the link between the chain and the spike which restricted Scuttles' movement. But it was just as well that they took the time, because when Eddie and Mo tried to lift the cot between them it was just too heavy. It was only when Scuttles had removed the strap from his ankle and come to help them that they were able to lift it off the ground.

They heaved and they puffed and they dragged the cot, and the babies cried all the way. They shushed them and sang to them, all in panicked whispers, but nothing would shut them up. Luckily everyone's attention in the cavern above was still drawn to the final few exchanges of the battle and they were able to slip out of the mouth of the cave and with one mighty final effort were able to load the cot into the back of the truck Mo had commandeered. Eddie and Mo climbed in with the babies, and did their best to secure the cot.

Whatever happened from here on in, they knew they were in for a rough ride.

Scuttles climbed behind the wheel and started the engine. He glanced back at them once. 'Fasten your seat belts,' he said, 'and prepare for take-off.'

Forty-One

Of all the people in that massive cavern, it was Alison Beech who spotted the lorry as it eased past the Crusher at a leisurely twenty miles an hour. Her eyes followed it for several moments. It wasn't because it was speeding, or because she could hear the babies – she couldn't – or indeed because she had spotted Scuttles behind the wheel – she hadn't. It was because it was out of place. Even though the Crusher had been attacked by weird, deformed creatures, even though it was damaged, even though most of her guards had taken off in angry pursuit of the creatures, she was aware of every last detail pertaining to her plan to crush the babies. That was what made her great, the leading businesswoman of her generation. While all hell was breaking loose around her, she was aware of a small truck being driven in an unremarkable fashion towards the road which led to the exit from Slieve Donard.

And it struck her as odd.

Then it struck her as worrying.

And finally it struck her like a thunderbolt.

The attack was a diversion which had drawn her best men away.

The lorry was what it was really all about.

She didn't even have to investigate – she knew instinctively that the babies were on board.

'Stop that lorry!' she screamed, with such violence that even the patrols setting out to track down the Forgotten hundreds of metres away turned in fear.

Those guards that remained close to her raced towards the lorry, drawing their weapons.

But the scream had alerted Scuttles as well.

He pressed his foot down hard on the accelerator and felt the lorry react enthusiastically. It leapt away across the cavern, leaving the guards trailing in its wake. It bounced energetically on to the twisting road which led to the exit. It rounded the corners at speed, its tyres taking a firm grip on the tarmac.

In the back Mo and Eddie used their feet to brace themselves against opposite walls while leaning their backs against the cot to keep it in place. They were thrown this way and that, but still managed to keep the cot steady.

'Are you okay back there?' Scuttles yelled.

'Fine!' shouted Mo.

'Just keep going!' yelled Eddie.

Scuttles took the lorry around the last bend before the security checkpoint and was relieved to see that the gate was raised and the hut used by the guards was on fire. The huge sliding door was slowly opening – he could see trees and sky beyond.

They were going to do it.

They were really going to do it.

As they raced past the burning checkpoint Scuttles caught a glimpse of something very strange indeed. A boy with three arms and just one eye in the dead centre of his forehead was saluting him. Scuttles shook his head. He hadn't eaten for a long time, it was clearly starting to affect him. He sped on, then glanced back in his mirror but there was no trace of his little hallucination.

Concentrate!

The doors were half open now.

Freedom lay beyond.

Scuttles gunned the lorry towards the widening gap, and they passed through it with a cheer.

They had done it.

They had escaped with the . . .

. . . and then a gunshot rang out and suddenly

he couldn't control the vehicle, it was swerving from side to side. A tyre had exploded. He tried to keep the lorry on the narrow mountain road but it was pulling to one side, towards the rocks that lined the road, he couldn't keep it straight, he couldn't keep it . . .

The lorry hit a rock, shot up over it and ploughed into the trees.

It careered through them for a hundred metres, smashing everything in its path, then shot out over a small dip and landed on its side with a frightening crash.

And then everything fell silent.

Even the birds were too shocked to sing.

It had been the wildest ride of Eddie's life. He had cracked his head a dozen times off the side of the lorry and now everything felt dizzy, woozy. He whispered, 'Mo . . . Mo . . .' but she was lying on her side, unconscious. He managed to grab hold of the top of the cot and drag himself up; he closed his eyes for a moment, fearing the worst, but then he heard a gentle cry. He opened his eyes and looked down at the twelve little babies. They were quite content, and not a hair on their heads, although some of them had no hair of course, had been harmed. Babies, they're tougher than you think, his mum had told him once.

Not like us.

His mum. He wondered if she was alive. He slumped back down. He wondered if his dad would ever come home or if he even had any idea that his son had been involved in such a dangerous adventure. Eddie forced his eyes to stay open. He looked towards the cab. He could see that the windscreen was smashed and the branch of a pine tree was jutting through the gap. Scuttles was slumped over the steering wheel.

Somewhere in the distance he could hear gunshots, and then even further away something like a helicopter, but it was all too much for him to work out. They'd come so close to escaping, so close to being heroes.

No – wait, they *were* heroes.

They had acted like heroes.

The only thing was, sometimes heroes died.

He didn't know if he was dying, but all he wanted to do was close his eyes. He wanted to sleep. Just a little sleep. He would wake up in time to die properly. But first just a little sleep.

Forty-Two

'Eddie?'

It was his dad's voice.

'Time to wake up, Eddie.'

'In a minute,' he said groggily. 'In a minute.'

He turned in the bed, trying to work out what day it was, whether he should be at school. No – it was the summer holidays. Back to sleep – yes, back to sleep. No panic about getting up.

'Eddie, come on.'

He'd been having a dream, something he couldn't remember. Somewhere there was a phone ringing, a baby crying, footsteps on linoleum. He smelled . . . disinfectant. Mum was cleaning again. That was it, she was a nurse, she knew what bugs could do. Eddie curled himself into a ball again. His dad could wait. Just for a while. His . . .

DAD!

Dad who had gone away without a word – Dad had come home!

Eddie tried to open his eyes, but they felt like they'd been taped shut. It was a real struggle, but he finally managed to open them a fraction and looked blurrily about him. He became aware of a figure standing at the end of his bed.

'Dad?'

'Yeah, you wish,' said the figure, and Eddie's eyes finally came into focus and saw Scuttles standing there wearing a neck brace and with both his arms in plaster. 'Time you got up and answered some questions, you lazy sod, I'm sick and tired of doing all the talking.'

'What are you on about?' Eddie asked. His voice was raspy dry. He pushed back the sheets on his bed and cautiously put his feet to the floor. Dizzy.

He was in a hospital that was for sure, and one glance out of the window told him it was the Royal Victoria. They were in a private room with just three beds. Scuttles was now sitting on one of them, while the other was empty but unkempt.

'Mo . . .' Eddie said quickly. 'Where's Mo?'

'Down the toilet,' snapped Scuttles and tried to point in their general direction, but winced instead at the pain in his arm. 'Just like my life,' he added needlessly.

Eddie rubbed at his brow. 'I don't understand . . . the babies . . . we crashed . . . I thought we were . . .'

'Dead,' finished Scuttles. 'So did I. And we very nearly were. That old bag Alison Beech was just about to have us shot when this bloody helicopter comes over the top of the mountain, full of police. And then about a hundred Land-Rovers come charging up the road, sirens wailing, and surround the lot of them.'

'You mean . . . ?'

'Yup, she's in prison.'

'And the babies . . . ?'

'Back with their parents.'

'And we're . . . ?'

'National bloody heroes.'

Eddie had been about to stand up, but stayed where he was on the side of the bed and took a deep breath.

'You're serious?'

'I'm always serious. Oh, the police'll spend the next few weeks questioning us about every detail, but they know they have the real baby-snatchers. We're off scot-free, lad.'

'But . . . how did they even know we were there?'

'That gang of troublemakers you hang around with tipped them off.'

'The . . . Reservoir Pups?'

'Yeah, whatever you call them.'

'But how did they know?'

'Look, this is all really boring, I'm sure you'll find out in due—'

'Just bloody tell me!'

Scuttles sighed. 'So your lot are a bit more sophisticated than I gave you credit for. When you broke into my office – and I haven't forgotten that and I will be pursuing you through the courts for burglary – you were wearing some kind of tracking device so that they could follow your progress. It seems you never took it off.'

Eddie blew air out of his cheeks. Then his brow furrowed: 'Does that mean they knew where I was all the time?'

Scuttles shrugged. 'Don't know, lad, you'll have to ask them that.'

At that moment the door opened and Mo came in. She had a can of Coke in each hand and didn't seem overly surprised to find him awake. But she smiled and showed him the cans. 'I brought you one. Unless you'd prefer Diet Coke.'

She raised an eyebrow.

Eddie was about to say something about the Forgotten, but she put a finger to her lips, then winked at him.

* * *

Six weeks later, a special ceremony was performed at the Royal Victoria Hospital. Many of the bigwigs who had attended Alison Beech on her previous visit were there, all of them saying that they had suspected she was involved all along, and all of them lying. They had no idea at all. Only Eddie had known, and then Mo and Scuttles.

The ceremony was to present medals for bravery to Eddie and Mo. Mum made him dress in his Sunday best. She hadn't been able to stop kissing him for the past few weeks. She called him 'My hero' around the house, and out in public, even while he was signing autographs, which really annoyed him.

Mo appeared wearing a dress, though she brought no relatives with her.

'You look very smart,' Mo said.

'And you look okay,' Eddie replied.

They were sitting at the front of a small hall, with about a hundred chairs ranged out behind them which were slowly filling up with local dignitaries and the parents and relatives of the stolen babies. Press photographers and television cameramen were setting up their equipment ready to record the ceremony.

Eddie really wasn't that interested. He was

thinking about the future. He turned to Mo. 'Were you serious?' he asked.

'What about?'

'What you were saying just before Alison Beech was going to have us squashed. About forming a gang. You and me.'

Mo shrugged. 'Suppose.'

'Okay,' said Eddie.

That was all they needed to say.

Eventually the speeches got under way and all kinds of praise was heaped upon Eddie and Mo and even Scuttles, who had been reinstated in his job and given a pay rise. Eddie's mum clapped loudly when Scuttles was presented with a special certificate for his part in the affair. Scuttles caught Eddie's eye and nodded at him. They had an agreement about Eddie's mum. Then Scuttles blew a special kiss to her. She went all red, then blew one back.

Eddie fumed.

'And now,' the Mayor of Belfast was saying, 'the presentation of the medals.'

Mo went up to get hers first, to loud applause.

Then Eddie's name was called, and the applause grew even louder.

When the medals had been pinned in place, the

Mayor returned to the microphone. 'As you will no doubt be aware, Alison Beech offered a reward of one million pounds for the return of the stolen babies. Now, she is in prison awaiting trial and really in no position to pay such a reward.' Gentle laughter rolled around the room. Eddie was sweating in his shirt and tie. He just wanted to be out of there. 'Her business empire is in tatters and her headquarters in Slieve Donard have been closed. All of the entrances to it have been sealed for ever.'

Eddie glanced at Mo. He had not mentioned the Forgotten to the police during any of the questioning. Neither had Mo. It wasn't their place. All they could do was hope that they had escaped from the mountain before it was closed. Mo nodded at him and reached for his hand. She squeezed it for a moment, and then let go.

'But the parents of these babies, together with several national newspapers and my own office, thought it was wrong that these brave children should go unrewarded. We have clubbed together, Eddie and Mo, and come up with this cheque for thirty thousand pounds as our way of saying thank you. You are real heroes.'

Eddie was lost for words. He didn't even move

to take the cheque. The Mayor folded it and thrust it into Eddie's top pocket, only pausing long enough to smile at the cameras as they exploded into life.

After the ceremony the crowd dispersed, the photographers took their final pictures, and Eddie stood with Mo planning their gang. Eddie's mum and Scuttles were looking at the cheque behind them.

'If he thinks he's getting any of that money,' Eddie hissed, 'he's got another thing coming.'

'Think what we can use it for,' Mo said. 'A proper headquarters, equipment, computers . . .'

'It's going to be great, Mo, we can really . . .'

And then he spotted Captain Black pushing his wheelchair towards them.

Eddie took a deep breath. He had been thrown out of the Reservoir Pups. Now he was probably going to be invited back. He glanced at Mo. He had promised to form a gang with her – but she was only one little girl, whereas the Pups had hundreds of members, real power.

He hated to let Mo down, but . . .

'Captain Black,' said Eddie as he approached, 'I just wanted to thank you for—'

But the leader of the Reservoir Pups rolled right past him, without so much as a nod of recognition.

He stopped instead in front of Eddie's mum. He held out his hand.

Eddie's mum hesitated for a moment, glanced at Eddie, then handed the cheque to Captain Black. He immediately put it in his pocket and pushed himself on past her and down the corridor towards the elevators.

What on earth had she done?

Eddie was so flabbergasted, he could hardly form the appropriate curse words to fire at his mother.

She came up to him and put an arm round his shoulders. 'I'm sorry, Eddie,' she said, 'I promised if there was any reward money, they could have it. They wouldn't have helped otherwise.'

Eddie glared after Captain Black's receding figure.

Join the Reservoir Pups?

Never in a million years.

He would build his own gang.

It might start out small, but with Mo's help, he would built the biggest, most fearsome outfit in the city. Then they'd sort out the Reservoir Pups. Good and proper.

* * *

THE END.

REALLY.

AT LEAST FOR NOW.